D0313770

About the author

NUALA NÍ CHONCHÚIR

lives in County Galway. She was chosen by *The Irish Times* as a writer to watch in 2009 and was recently shortlisted for the European Prize for Literature. Nuala was one of four winners of the Templar Poetry Pamphlet and Collection competition. Her poetry pamphlet *Portrait of the Artist with a Red Car* was published by Templar in November 2009. Her third short fiction collection *Nude* was published by Salt Publishing in September 2009. Nuala was awarded Arts Council Bursaries in 2004 and 2009. She has poems and an essay in *The Watchful Heart – A New Generation of Irish Poets*, edited by Joan McBreen (Salmon, 2009). A new collection of poetry, *The Juno Charm*, will be published by Templar in November 2010.

www.nualanichonchuir.com

YOU

Also by

NUALA NÍ CHONCHÚIR

Short Fiction

Nude
To The World of Men, Welcome
The Wind Across the Grass

Poetry

Portrait of the Artist With a Red Car
Tattoo: Tatú
Molly's Daughter

Plays: Co-author

Departures

LIBRARIES NI
WITHDRAWN FROM STOCK

YOU

NUALA
NÍ CHONCHÚIR

YOU
First published 2010
by New Island
2 Brookside
Dundrum Road
Dublin 14

www.newisland.ie

Copyright © Nuala Ní Chonchúir

The author has asserted her moral rights.

ISBN 978-1-84840-063-4

All rights reserved. The material in this publication is protected by copyright law. Except as may be permitted by law, no part of the material may be reproduced (including by storage in a retrieval system) or transmitted in any form or by any means; adapted; rented or lent without the written permission of the copyright owner.

British Library Cataloguing Data. A CIP catalogue record for this book is available from the British Library.

Book design by Inka Hagen

Printed in the UK by CPI Mackays, Chatham ME5 8TD.

10 9 8 7 6 5 4 3 2 1

LIBRARIES NI	
C700805580	
RONDO	27/10/2011
F	£ 11.50
CLL	

For Ma, Da and all the Mill Laners

ACKNOWLEDGEMENTS

My thanks go to Jonathan Williams; Deirdre O'Neill and Elaina O'Neill at New Island; The Arts Council for a bursary; my writing group, The Peers; Karen O'Neill for photos; Órfhlaith Foyle for her belief; my parents and family; Finbar McLoughlin; John Dillon; Cúán and Finn Dillon; Juno McLoughlin.

BOOK ONE

1

Anything Strange Or Startling?

Your ma used up all the juice again. Last week you asked could she get two cartons of orange from now on, instead of only one, because there was never any for you and your brother Liam. She went mad, shouting at you so much that you could see frothy bits at the sides of her mouth, like the scurf that Liam calls Guinness water that floats on the top of the river.

'Do you think I'm made of money? Do you think I'm Rockefeller?' she roared. She lost the cool with you for ten minutes.

'OK, OK, I was only saying.'

She called you a cheeky pup and said to get out of her sight.

There's no juice left because your ma knocked it back with her drink again. That means you have to get Liam ready for school and he'll keep saying 'I want Mammy'. You like a drop of orange in the morning. Even though it makes your throat creamy, it's refreshing. It goes well with toast and marmalade. You don't drink tea any more. You gave it up two years ago when you were eight. First you stopped having sugar in your tea and then you decided not to drink it ever again. You think you feel better for it. Your ma loves a nice cup of tea. She likes it strong; strong enough to dry her mouth. Weak tea is piss-water, she says, but she doesn't say it in front of visitors, only to you and her friend Cora.

Cora is huge and has hands that are knotted like a bird's claws. Your ma doesn't mind; she thinks Cora is a marvel. She calls her a girl, but really she must be about fifty. Cora's husband, Noel, is a lousy eejit. He has a preggy belly and sideburns like sweeping brushes. The state of him, your ma says, and Cora laughs, but then sometimes she doesn't laugh. Sometimes she's in love with Noel.

You and Liam play 'Cora': you pick up your cups of milk with claw hands and say 'Indeed and it is' and 'Indeed and it does' and 'Anything strange or startling?' That's the way Cora goes on. Your ma caught you at it before. 'Stop that, you brats,' she said, but she laughed.

You make a cup of tea for your ma and bring it up to her bedroom. It smells like dirty tights and talc in there in the mornings and the air is always warm. Your ma's head is sticking out of the sheets and her cheeks are rosy. The baby lies beside her with dribbles falling from his mouth. Your ma's pink cheeks are called grog blossoms – her and Cora say that – and she only gets them when she's after having a drink. She covers them with foundation if she has to go anywhere. She is so pale the rest of the time that you like her grog blossoms because they make her look happy. She was crying again last night.

'A cup of tea for you,' you whisper and she pulls herself up, groaning.

The baby is asleep beside her in the bed; he's one and a bit but he still won't sleep in a cot.

'Leave it there, like a good girl,' she says, pointing to the bedside table. She squeezes your hand and tries to give you a kiss, but you turn your head to one side because of the sour smell of her mouth. She drops your hand and pushes you away.

'Go on so, Little Miss Prim,' she says.

On the landing you stop to look out at the river rushing below the window. Your house is special: it's built right on top of the river. The river wall is your wall. You've had two floods, but your ma doesn't want to move. She won't live in one of those matchboxes up in the town, she says, not for love or money.

You get Liam's breakfast ready and then pull him out of bed.

His hair is all over the place, so you brush it down while he's eating. You do your own hair then and leave the hairbrush back on the counter for Ma. The brush has three types of hair stuck in it: yours, your ma's and Liam's. The baby's hair is so short it doesn't need brushing yet, and anyway, it's sort of knobbly and curly, so it wouldn't brush properly. Having to clean out Liam's lunchbox before you can put the lunch in delays you. That means you're late for meeting Gwen and it's the last day of school before the summer holidays and she'll walk on without you. Gwen is your best friend on earth. She's Welsh and some day, she always says, she'll be leaving Dublin to go back there. Gwen says that Wales is much better than Ireland and that she's pure British because her mother is Scottish and her dad is English, but *she* was born in Wales. You say you are pure Irish, but she says that doesn't cut any ice with her because so are most people in Ireland. You hope she never goes back to Wales.

Sure enough, Gwen is gone on ahead by the time you get down past the row of houses and the bridge over the river where you always meet her. You just hope she hasn't walked to school with Anne. That Anne is always trying to steal Gwen away. You'd love to give Anne a good bite on the cheek or something like that. She has fat lips and blonde hair and her family is rich. She wears a red kilt with a big curly pin in it and you'd like a kilt like that. She has a room full of medals and trophies for Irish dancing. You wish bad things would happen to her, but sometimes you feel guilty because your granny used to say that, in the eyes of God, thinking a bad thing is as bad as doing it. You're not sure you believe that. Since your granny died, you don't have to go to Mass any more. Your ma says that the priests have too much old blether. Mass is boring and, anyway, everyone just sits there with their minds wandering, pretending to be holy.

Your granny was ancient. She died in the home and the nurses wouldn't let her have her fags, which were her one pleasure. She used to say that the nurses were stealing her money.

'I'd a half-crown under my pillow this morning and now it's gone,' she'd say.

'Half-crowns went out with the Ark, Granny,' you'd say, but she'd just nod and clack her false teeth against her gums and tell you to keep saying your prayers.

At school, before the teacher comes in, they're all going on about the volcano that erupted in America. It's Mount St Helens this and Mount St Helens that, as if any of them had ever been there. Still, you get swept away with all the talk about the volcano and next thing you know you're saying that your uncle lives in Washington in a big wooden house. They're all looking at you.

'Yes,' you say, 'he saw the whole thing. He heard it going off and in the morning the smoke had blotted out the sun. And then molten lava flowed right past his door, killing dogs and people and everything.'

'How do *you* know?' asks Anne.

'Because he rang us up right when it was happening.'

'I didn't know youse had a telephone,' she says, real sly.

'They just got one in,' says Gwen, saving your neck.

That Anne is a greasy cow; you hate her flabby mouth. On the way home, Gwen asks if you really have an uncle in Washington and you say that you have, keeping up the lie even though she's your best friend. Your face is going red, so you tell her that your ma went out with a fella called Eugene on Saturday night.

'They went to the pictures to see *The Elephant Man*. Ma said it was morbid and she nearly fell asleep. She said, "What kind of a gobshite brings a woman to see a film like that?"'

Gwen laughs. 'A big gobshite,' she says. Then she says that she has something to tell you. She's going away with her mam and dad. 'Back to Wales – out of this place at last,' she says.

You can't believe it – she seems so happy! You shuffle along beside her.

'We're going away too,' you say after a minute. She asks where. 'We're going to Washington, if you must know,' you say, very loud. She looks at you sideways. Then you run off home because you think you're going to cry.

The front door is locked and it's Cora who opens it. 'There you are,' she says, her hook hands curved into her chest. 'Anything strange or startling?' Her voice is funny and she's looking over your head instead of at your face.

You go into the kitchen; Noel is there and you ask where your ma is. He doesn't lift his head from his dinner.

'Ah, now,' says Cora, still not looking at you, 'she's had to take a trip for herself. Noel and me are going to mind the three of you until she's able to get back.'

'What kind of a trip? Where to?'

Cora looks over at Noel. 'Well, she's gone into the hospital, to Saint Angela's; she just had to go in for a little rest.'

'Saint Angela's is for old people.'

'Yes…well, it was the nearest.'

Cora picks up a cloth and starts wiping at nothing. Liam is at the table. The baby's in his high-chair; there's stuff stuck all over his face. Noel is sitting in your ma's chair, scoffing chips.

'Come on, love,' he grunts, 'sit down there now and have your dinner.'

You can see all the mashed-up chips through his teeth.

'I'm not your love,' you say and you go up to your room.

Your ma looks as pale as buttermilk when you visit her in the hospital, even paler than usual. She's wearing a paper nightdress and it rustles when she shifts in the bed. There's a smell in the ward like clean on top of dirty, and the old women in the beds stare at you when Cora brings you and Liam and the baby in. One of them calls you over, but she's talking gibberish and you can't understand a word she says. She tries to pet the baby's cheek, but he wriggles away and puts his face into your shoulder. Liam giggles. Your ma's eyes are all puffy and red. Her arms are flopped in front of her. They are in bits, covered in trails of brown scabs that have high pink sides. Liam puts his finger on the cuts. She touches his cheek and he starts to cry.

'There now, little pudding,' she says, but she is nearly crying too. She takes the flowers you've brought and sniffs them, except they are chrysanthemums and they have no real smell. 'They're gorgeous, kids, thanks,' she says very quietly.

'Indeed and they are, Joan,' says Cora and she pats Liam on the head with her crabby hand. He pulls his head away, tossing his hair. Joan is what your ma's called, like Joan of Arc, but she was French – your ma is only Irish.

Your ma has nothing to say for herself and it's hard to know what to talk about. She cuddles the baby and he paws at her nightie, trying to get at her boobs. The baby drinks milk from your ma's boobs; it's called breastfeeding. He still gets suckies, even though he is more than a year old, has teeth, can eat biscuits and is walking by himself. Your ma always says that breast is best and you'll all be brainboxes thanks to her. Cora tells her the death toll from the volcano in America has reached fifty-eight and that Noel is gone in to have his corns pared. Your ma doesn't say anything; she just stares at you all and hugs the baby. It's like as if she's asleep but awake at the same time. You tell her that Gwen and her mam and dad are going back to Wales. She nods. You want her to say something about the school holidays and Gwen leaving, but you can tell she's miles away.

'This place is stinky,' says Liam; 'it smells like bums.'

You give him a puck to shut him up, but your ma laughs.

'You're right, Liam,' she says and you all laugh, but Cora laughs a bit too hard.

'It's not that funny,' you say and she stops.

'I'll just go and ask the nurse for a vase for the flowers,' she says.

'Well?' whispers your ma when she's gone.

'Well,' Liam says, 'what happened to your arms?'

'I had an accident. I was attacked by a lawnmower.' She smiles.

Liam stares at her all gawpy-eyed. 'Noel won't let us watch what we want to on the telly.'

'When are you getting out?' you ask.

'I'll be out next week and we'll go to the zoo, just the four of us.'

The last time you all went to the zoo, she met a fella and you ended up in a pub on Parkgate Street for the rest of the day, with her doing false laughs and him grabbing at her. Afterwards she called him a mean little scut because he didn't give you all a lift home.

'Not the zoo,' you say.

She moves in the bed, cradling the baby across her lap, and reaches over to her locker. 'I've a few sweets in here.'

She can't pull the door open. Her hospital nightdress has no back to it and her grey bra strap is on view. You rush round the bed to help her open the door, so she'll sit back and not be making a show of you all. She's still stretching.

'Oh feck!' she yelps, holding on to her arm. One of her cuts has opened and big globs of blood are sliding down her wrist onto the bedspread. The baby claps his hands. Cora comes down the ward and then runs off screaming 'Nurse! Nurse!' as if someone is choking to death. The nurse comes and says it would be best if your ma rested, cutting the visit short. Cora pushes you out of the place, hardly giving you a chance to say goodbye. All the old ladies start waving, thinking you've been in to visit them.

'The poor creatures,' says Cora, too loud.

After a week, your ma comes home and says she just wants to be left in peace for a while. You feel like being on your own too, so you go out for a walk along the river, taking the baby with you.

The river is your favourite place, but you can't seem to get in the mood for it, so you turn around and push the pram up by the shops. You take your time – that's what Cora calls dawdling – and the baby is happy in his pram. There's nothing much to see and after a while you head back home.

When you get to the house, Liam is lashing a football at the front wall. He doesn't look at you when you say 'Hello, smelly'. You let yourself in the side gate that leads into the yard and then through to the kitchen. Your ma is buckled again, sitting at the table with a bottle of vodka, spilling some of it when she pours in more. The baby sees your ma and gurgles. You take him out of the pram and let him down on the floor.

'I thought you weren't supposed to drink because you're on those tablets,' you say.

'You,' she slurs, 'you're the cause of it all.'

You hate when she's like this. 'Go to bed, Ma, and give me that bottle.'

She jumps up and lunges at you. 'Get off my lip!' she screams into your face, grabbing at your clothes. 'I wish none of youse had ever been born.'

You run into the sitting room, then up to your own room and shut the door. You lie on the bed thinking about the volcano in Washington, thinking that it might be easier to live over there than here, until you fall asleep. When you wake up, it's dark and the house is quiet. All you can hear is the shush-hush of the weir as the river water topples over it on its way to the sea.

2

A Different Daddy

The baby has a different daddy to you and Liam. You don't know who he is because your ma won't say. Her and Cora were talking about him one day and you asked what his name was and your ma said, 'His name is Santy Claus.' Then the pair of them burst out laughing. The baby is your half-brother, but you don't say that out loud because it sounds a bit mean. Anyway, he feels like a full brother to you – just like Liam. You love the baby; he has a mad, happy laugh and lovely brown skin.

But you wish your ma wouldn't give him suckies when your friend is in the house. Even though Gwen doesn't seem to mind, you feel mortified when your ma displays herself. Her boobs have blue veins but her nipples and all around them are brown. Gwen likes to watch the baby having his milk and she asks your ma does it hurt and when will she stop breastfeeding. Gwen has no brothers or sisters and she'd like one. One day she said that her dad told her that hedgehogs can suck milk from a cow's boobs, which are called udders. You would love to see that for yourself and you wonder if the hedgehog would have to jump up to get its little mouth around the cow's nipple. Your ma said that she thought that might be only an old wives' tale, but you'd never know.

You don't see your da a lot. He left when you were only seven, so for three years you have been without him. He has a girlfriend called Geraldine and a child now, a half-sister for you, but you don't know her very well. She doesn't feel like a real sister because you don't even remember her name, except sometimes. They all live a long way away on the Northside and you would have to get a bus or maybe even a train to their house. And anyway they live in a flat and your ma says it's a Corporation flat and she wouldn't be caught dead in it, thank you very much. Then she says 'Hasn't he done well for himself?' and she does her angry laugh, but she only goes on like that when she's had a drink. Really you know that your half-sister is called Clare, like the county; you just pretend to yourself that you don't.

You don't even miss your da much because he used to work in foreign countries fixing electricity or something, so you don't remember him being around the house anyway. Once every couple of months he asks to meet you and Liam but not the baby, and your ma brings you into town on the bus and leaves you outside Eason's. Then he comes and brings you to Fusciardi's or wherever for chips and you have to answer all his dopey questions. Your da's name is Willy, but if anyone asks, you say his name is William. Liam is called Liam after him but he isn't called Willy, thank God.

'So,' he says, 'has your ma nabbed herself a new fella yet?'

'No.'

'How's school?'

'Grand.'

'Are you good at your lessons? Are you good for the teacher?'

'Yeah.'

He asks the exact same things every time. Then he gives you a pound note each and says not to spend it all in the one shop and he gives you an envelope for your ma. He buys sweets from the pick 'n' mix, a bag each. Liam is always quiet until it's time to go and then he starts bawling as if he's crazy about your da. By the time you meet your ma again, Liam is sobbing and hiccupping like a loony. You tell your ma the way he carries on and the things your da says, and you can see that she's pleased because she's nice to Liam on the bus on the way home.

Your ma loves to go to the pictures and before the baby came you all used to go, and Cora too sometimes. But since the time the man kicked you all out there's no point bringing the baby any more. You wouldn't mind only the baby wasn't making any noise; your man must've been hearing things. When you all got out into the foyer, Cora, who was with you that day, asked him if he'd had his affliction long. And when he said 'What affliction would that be, Madam?' she said 'Pain-in-the-hole-itis!' You went scarlet, but you thought fair play to her, because there was no need to throw you all out when the baby was having his suckies in the cinema and was as quiet as the grave. Your ma said the cinema fella had had it in for her for ages because he'd asked her out once and she'd said no.

'Imagine that scrawny effort thinking he'd get the likes of you!' said Cora, and your ma linked Cora's bent-up arm in her own while you carried the baby on your hip, and you all headed off for the bus. 'And,' said Cora, 'he can shove his poxy popcorn up his you-know-where!' and you all laughed. That made the baby laugh, although he didn't really understand.

Your ma likes films and television and the newspaper. Cora brings the paper around when Noel has gone through it from cover to cover. Noel is a coalman and he has a phlegmy cough. That's a word you hate, phlegmy, because it sounds like what it is: thick, green and snotty. Noel has black dirt under his fingernails that makes you sick and, like you, he's always reading, but he only likes the paper and detective novels; you will read anything. Your ma reads the newspaper from back to front because she is a *citeog*, which means she does everything with her left hand, including reading.

Your ma says, 'What's black and white and red all over?'

'A penguin who's been run over,' you say.

'A nun who's been run over,' says Liam.

'No, a newspaper!' says your ma. It took you ages to get that one.

Noel doesn't like *The Irish Times.* He says it's a Proddy newspaper and then he says 'Up the Republic!' and Cora says 'Will you stop that codology.' Cora says things like that because she's a culchie. But she hates being called that. 'I'm from inside the Pale,' she says, as if that matters. You say that Kildare is not the centre of the universe and she says it is for some people.

Cora and Noel are in your house drinking with your ma and eating all the food, as usual. They sit yacking on about *Dallas* and who shot J.R. and the price of this, that and the other. Then they all light up fags and you can hardly see in front of you with the smoke coming off them. Cora says she'd be like a demon without her Major and she looks weird dragging on the cigarette with her claw hands, not cool like the women in the films. You and Liam cough and cough.

'Get out if you don't like it and bring the baby with you,' your ma says.

Then you are stuck minding the baby and can't go out to hang around with Gwen, who'll be leaving any day now. The baby doesn't want to do anything you want to do and he cries until his whole face is full of snots and he's all sweaty and hot. Sometimes you feel sorry for him, but other times you just think he's a pain.

'If you put him in the pram and go for a walk, he might fall asleep,' your ma says, meaning get out and leave us in peace.

You put on the baby's coat. His arms get caught in the sleeves and he starts to roar, but you stuff his soother in his mouth and he's OK again. Liam wants to come with you but you're calling to Gwen's house, so you say no; he has no friends and he's always following you around, mortifying you in front of Gwen. His hair is a disaster, sticking up all over the place, and he picks his nose and the scabs on his knees. You only pick your nose when no one is looking, like in your room at night, and it can be very satisfying.

Your ma says you have to bring Liam with you and that really annoys you.

'What did your last slave die of?' you ask her. 'Exhaustion?'

Your ma doesn't take kindly to that and she throws her shoe across the room at you, but she misses, accidentally on purpose.

'Get out, you pup!' she roars but she's not really cross, you can tell.

So you drag Liam and the baby with you down past the bridge to Gwen's house. You notice that the river is very high and is flowing fast, even though it hasn't been raining. When you get to Gwen's house, her mam opens the door and says 'Oh look – the whole gang,' real smart. Gwen is in her room listening to Kate Bush on her transistor.

Your ma looks like Kate Bush only older. Everyone says it. She has wavy hair. You wish you had hair like that, but you've obviously got your da's hair: mousy, straight and in rats' tails. That's what your ma says, that your hair is like rats' tails. She says it in a way that makes you know there's nothing you can do about it. It's not very nice. Cora looks a little bit like Nana Mouskouri, who is Greek and wears big glasses. Cora wears them kind of glasses when she reads the paper and Noel calls her 'Nana' as a joke. That drives Cora mental.

Kate Bush sings 'Babooshka' and she does waily bits like yaaah-yaaah. Liam sits on the floor looking at Gwen's books, the baby stays asleep in the pram and you and Gwen sing along to the radio. You have a nice voice. Your ma can't sing a note, but that doesn't stop her, especially when she's had a few jars. She sings Simon and Garfunkel songs and they're always a bit sad. Noel sings Elvis and he pretends to have a microphone even when everyone is looking at him. He fancies himself as Elvis with his too-small-for-him leather jacket and manky sideburns. He wishes he was him, even though Elvis is dead. When Noel sings, you think it's lucky your house is not stuck onto any other houses.

Your cousin Rory is in a band called Neighbourhood Disturbance, but you don't know if they're any good. Your auntie Bridget gave them that name. She's older than your ma and very lah-di-dah. Your ma used to call her Miss Prim and now she calls you Little Miss Prim, but you hope you're not like your auntie because she's always in a bad mood. Your ma says that she has a face like a well-slapped arse.

Your cousin Rory is fifteen. He told you once that he loved you. He only said it because he had you as a prisoner in his room and he tried to stick his tongue into your mouth. He held down your arms but you got away. Now you avoid him because he makes you feel weird. He laughs every time he sees you and he calls you a sap. Rory's big thing is music. You like music too and you listen to Radio Dublin on your transistor in bed at night. All the people write in and you wish you could do that too, but you never do.

You and Gwen love the Eurovision. She supported Ireland this time – even though she's pure British – because Johnny Logan was in it and he's gorgeous. Prima Donna were in it for Britain but they didn't stand a chance because Johnny is the business. And he won!

'I might marry Johnny when I grow up,' says Gwen.

'Oh, he'll want to marry an Irish person,' you say and she gets real sulky.

'I might be back in Ireland by then.'

'I thought you couldn't wait to get out of Ireland,!' you say.

'Well, I can't,' she shouts in your face, 'and you can go home now and bring your stinky brothers with you!'

You pull Liam off the floor and drag the pram out the door, banging it behind you to make a point.

It's getting dark as you walk home. Liam dawdles along picking dandelions for your ma. She calls them piss-the-beds, but Liam doesn't know that and he thinks they're lovely, so you just let him collect bunches of them. Liam always wets the bed after you've been to see your da. Your ma has to put a black plastic bag under the sheet because the mattress is destroyed. You used to wet the bed too and it feels nice and warm when you do it, but then it gets cold and there's a wissy smell and you can't get back to sleep. That's when you have to tell your ma what's after happening.

Sometimes Liam tries to get into your bed with you when he's wet his own, but you don't want his piddly pyjamas in your bed, so you bring him in to your ma. The odd time she gets really angry, but other times she just tells him to strip off and hop in beside her and the baby. The baby sleeps in with your ma, all cuddly and warm. It would be nice to be in there too, you think.

3

Friends

Your house is full of creepy-crawlies and some of them have horrible wiggling legs, but you like the look of them anyway, just not to touch. The only ones you'll touch are ladybirds, butterflies and hairy mollies. A butterfly lives on your windowsill. Ladybirds are your favourite; they crawl around on your hand until you tell them to fly away home because their house is on fire and their children are gone. Cora taught you how to say that and you like it, even though it was her that taught you. Sometimes a ladybird will do a little yellow poo on your hand and it smells sour, but they only do that when they're afraid. You don't mind daddy-long-legs, even though they make scuttly noises when they run across the wall, but you hate woodlice. One of them is called a louse; loads are called lice. They fall onto their backs and wiggle their millions of grey legs, and they can run very fast. They crunch when you squash them and that makes you feel sick. Sometimes there's a louse in the bath and you have to call your ma to get rid of it and rinse the bath out before you'll get in.

Once, at school, you got the other kind of lice in your hair. Even though they only latch on to clean hair, it makes you feel dirty because your head gets real itchy. Your ma doesn't like when you bring them home on your head because then she has to use the fine comb and the stinky shampoo and it takes ages to kill the little bastards. That's what your ma says, but she does a good job of it and she shows you all their corpses lying on the newspaper when she's done.

Cora comes to tell you that your da will be ringing at six o'clock.

He phones Cora and Noel's house and you have to walk over there to talk to him. It's not far but you hate it because there's no privacy with Noel hawing down your neck pretending not to listen, and Cora humming and banging in the kitchen doing the same. Their house smells like the inside of a pub – damp and smoky and old. They don't have any kids and when you asked Cora about that, her lips went into a tortoise-mouth shape and she said it was none of your concern, and anyway, she asked, what would she do with a rake of snotty-nosed brats?

You sit in the hall waiting for the phone to ring. It's already ten past six and you're getting fed up, but eventually it rings. Your da sounds different on the phone than he does in real life, like he has a cold or is a hundred miles away. You wouldn't care if he was.

'How's school?' he asks.

'Fine. We're on holidays now.'

'Good, good.'

'We started doing geography this year. The Shannon is the longest river in Ireland.'

'Is that so?' he says, trying to sound really interested.

'Yes, but the Liffey is better.'

He laughs. 'Well, guess what?' he says then. You don't know what to guess. 'Myself and Geraldine are going to have another baby.'

'Oh.'

'Another brother or sister for yourself and Liam.' Big deal, you think. Then there's silence, just the humming of the phone line. You wonder if there are any crossed lines, if there are people listening to the silence and wondering if there's anyone there at all. 'Well,' says your da, 'isn't that great news altogether?'

'Oh, yeah, another half-brother or -sister,' you say to sting him, but he doesn't answer that.

'How's your ma?' he asks.

'Grand,' you answer and that's that.

When you're finished on the phone, you thank Cora like your ma always says to, and she asks if your da had any news. You tell her about the baby and she says that he can't keep his powder dry, that fella. Noel says he'd be better off keeping himself to himself and Cora tells him to shush.

You run home along by the river and you can hear it gurgling and splashing. You pick some of the pink and the white valerian that grows in clumps on the river wall for your ma. Even though Rory says that they make dangerous drugs from valerian, you think they look nice, not like dandelions.

When you get home, you tell your ma about your da's new baby and she laughs. She laughs so much that in the end she gets the hiccups. You stare at her and after a while she waves you away and says not to tell Liam, which you weren't going to do anyway because he couldn't care less about babies. Your ma says that your da will get his come-uppance.

Your da is an electrician – he calls himself a 'sparks'. That's his word for himself and he's proud of it. You don't want any more babies in your life. All they do is cry and poo and have suckies. But the baby you have is nice; he has brown skin and is small and squishy, and he smells good most of the time. You really love the baby.

You saw a black man before. He was a priest, even though he was young, and he came to your school and talked all about Africa. His skin was blue-black and you wanted to touch his cheeks because they looked shiny and firm. The palms of his hands were light brown, like the baby's skin, and you could see the creases on them.

Gwen says her cousins in Manchester are black, but you know she's lying because her and her mam and dad are white, as white as you. She says 'mam and dad' and not 'ma and da' because she is Welsh. When you get married and have babies, you're going to have one black baby and one Chinese baby and one Red Indian baby. Indians are very handsome and noble. They live in America and they wear feathers in their hair and you like that. If you wore feathers in your hair in Ireland, everyone would think you were a loony-tune. Soldiers killed the Red Indians and took their land. When your ma is angry, she says she's going to run off with a soldier, but she doesn't know any soldiers, so you don't think she will. Your da used to be a soldier, though, when he was younger.

The kitchen is alive with mice and your ma is doing her nut. They are leaving their little poo pellets in the food press and are chewing on the Weetabix box.

'I'll kill every bastarding one of them!' she screams, running around banging at the press with her sweeping brush.

'Well, at least it's not rats,' you say, reminding her of the time the house got flooded and when you came back after staying in Cora's there were rats in the hot press making nests out of the spare blankets. But you're sorry you said anything because your ma has a thing about rats and she gets sarky with you and starts to screech. 'Oh, well, thank God for that. It's only an invasion of mice,' she yelps. 'Only a bloody army of ten thousand shagging mice!'

Your ma has the same nightmare over and over. She dreams there's a big white rat living under the bathroom floor and that when she's on the pot, he jumps up and sinks his fangs into her bum. She always wakes up then, but says she can feel him biting through her skin and she feels choky as she comes out of the dream. Whenever she sees a real rat, she freezes and gets a scaldy red rash on her neck. You're not fond of rats yourself – they look evil – but mice are OK and the smallest ones are very sweet looking. You hate when your ma sets traps all over the place and the little furry mice are nearly cut in half in them, all for the love of a piece of cheese. Sometimes you hear the traps going off in the night and you're sure you can hear the mouse squeaking before it dies. But still you don't want mice running over your pillow in the night or catching in your hair. They are OK to look at, but you don't want to feel one on your skin.

Gwen calls to your door as if nothing had happened and you hadn't huffed out of her house after she'd told you to go. You can't believe your eyes because Anne is with her. You stand sideways, half-in and half-out of the house, holding on to the front door so that they can't come in. You would have let Gwen in, but you don't want Anne in your house because it's in a mess and your ma is still raving on about the mice. They stand back a bit and Gwen asks if you're coming out. You say no. She has a silly smile on her face, and her and Anne keep whispering and laughing about something.

'Who's at that door?' your ma asks, coming and pulling it open. She looks a bit mad with her bushy hair all over the place and she's swinging the sweeping brush around.

'Hello, Mrs Dunne,' says Gwen.

'Mrs Dunne!' your ma humphs. 'I wasn't christened "Mrs Dunne". Call me Joan, girls.' She laughs and goes back to the kitchen.

Gwen and Anne start sniggering again and pucking each other with their elbows.

'I love your dress,' says Anne, and Gwen goes into convulsions. You look down at your dress. It has green and yellow flowers all over it and a row of buttons at the neck and you think it's OK. You're only wearing it because your trousers are in the wash; it's not really good for messing around in. It came in a bag with loads of other clothes from Cora's niece, who is older than you. You stare at Gwen. You know she's only going on like this because Anne is with her. She won't catch your eye, but her laugh trails away.

'Do you want to come in?' you ask after a while. You don't really relish the thought of Anne looking at your furniture, which is old, and at your bedroom, which smells like stale runners, even though you have an Air Wick.

'No,' Anne says. 'I'm not allowed in your house, since your mother … well, since your mother was in the loony bin.'

'She wasn't in the loony bin! She was in hospital.' Your face feels hot and you know your neck is getting blotches. 'When are you going back to Wales?' you say to Gwen, to change the subject.

'She *was* in the loony,' Anne says. 'Everyone at school knows. Gwen told us that she tried to top herself.'

Gwen stares at you, brazen, and you get furious, so you slam the door in their faces. You're breathing very loud, like a horse, and the sound muffles your ears. Then you go to the window and watch the two of them through the lace curtain as they run off. You're sure you can hear them laughing and you vow never to have another friend because it's not worth the bother.

The baby is strapped into his pram in the sitting room, eating a Liga; all the brown bits of it are smushed into his face and clothes. Your ma is still banging around the kitchen after the mice and she's using the F-word, so things are getting really bad. You hope she doesn't decide to take a drink after all the excitement of hunting out the mice. She comes into the sitting room and asks if your friends are gone; there's a tea towel wrapped around her head. She is carrying the sweeping brush handle like a sword; the brush bit is broken off it and there are splinters sticking out of the end.

'Yes, if you must know, they *are* gone,' you shout. 'All thanks to you!'

You run out and up the stairs and she follows you. You're in such a hurry that you trip, but you manage to get up again quickly. You hurt your knee but you don't stop to rub it because that would only give her the satisfaction of knowing you were in pain.

'Go on, so, narky-hole,' she shouts after you and then she starts to laugh.

You wish that your room had a lock because then you could

lock yourself in. You have the best room in the house – one of your windows looks out on to the river from high up and you can see the weir as well as down the other way which is towards the sea. The butterfly who lives in your room likes to cling to the net curtains for days on end and all you can see are the powdery backs of her wings. Sometimes you think she is dead for sure, but when you go right down beside her you can see her tiny feelers moving. You put on a tape and dance around real noisy for a while to annoy your ma, but then you're afraid of disturbing the butterfly, so you stop.

You take out the shoebox – where you keep your Sindy dolls – from the bottom of the wardrobe. You have four of them – one dark, one blonde, one with red hair and one with a piece of black fur glued to her head where her hair used to be. You got the last one at a sale of work and someone else had already cut her hair short, so you just put the fur on as something different. It was meant to be an afro but it looks kind of stupid. Anyway, that one is the man Sindy in your games because Liam won't part with his Action Man; you'd think he was in love with him or something. You play Sindys for a while, changing their clothes and making them kiss and have fights with the man-Sindy.

You wonder if your ma will ever fall in love again the way your da has. Even if she does, you hope she doesn't have any more babies, especially not with Eugene, who is ugly. You would like a sister who could live with you in your house, but you're not desperate for one. Clare is only a half-sister and she lives so far away. The best thing would be to have a sister near your own age, but it's too late for that.

You're a bit big for dolls, but you don't mind the odd go of the Sindys. After a while it gets boring and you can't think of anything else for them to say or do, so you pack them back into the shoebox and put it into the wardrobe, behind your clothes.

You sneak out onto the landing and listen, but all you can hear is the ordinary sounds from outside of cars and kids playing. And the river. The house is quiet.

4

A Party

You've all been invited to Noel's party. He'll be forty, which you find surprising – in your opinion he looks much older than that. It was supposed to be a surprise party, but Cora says she's sure some eejit of a coalman who works with him let the cat out of the bag and she could kill him. Noel's dropping hints like bombs, so Cora knows that he knows.

'I'm sorry I ever started it, Joan,' she moans to your ma, sucking on her fag and blowing the smoke all around the kitchen when you're trying to eat some dinner in peace. You wave your hands to make the smoke go away.

'Ah, it'll be great,' says your ma. 'How often do we get a chance to let our hair down, Cora? I'll help you. We'll make salmon sandwiches and ones with egg and onion. Everyone likes them.' You make a face and your ma says she'll give you a clip around the ear if you don't behave. 'I'll leave you here to mind your brothers,' she says, 'and you'll go to no party. How would you like that?'

You wouldn't like that. Even though it's only Noel, you are delighted to be going to a proper big people's party. 'Would you not leave the kids out of it altogether, Cora, and have it adults only?' your ma says, but she's looking sideways at you and you know she's only trying to get up your nose. Cora specifically invited you and Liam and the baby because she says you're like family and Noel would be awful upset if you weren't there.

'Ah now, we don't want to disappoint Noel on his special day,' says Cora with a big grin at you. You smile back, even though she's licking up to you.

Your ma sends you down to Cora and Noel's house early on the day of the party to help with the tidying up. Cora can't do everything with her hands being riddled with arthritis and all, so your ma says you'll dig in and Cora's delighted. All the windows are open when you get there and the place smells decent for once. Cora's in the kitchen mixing up dough for the apple tarts. She holds the wooden spoon in her claw and the bowl under her arm and she's really good at it. She has a fag in the corner of her mouth and the smoke is making her eyes drip.

'Ah, there you are, good girl. Now, there's a tin of Mr Sheen and a duster in that press. You get cracking on the sitting room.'

You don't mind dusting. Your ma never really does it at home and you like the smell of the polish. Plus you get to have a goo through Cora and Noel's shelves without anyone saying you're nosy. You decide to polish all the ornaments without even being asked. Cora calls them old gewgaws, but she keeps them for sentimental reasons; like the photograph of Bray that's in a frame made entirely of seashells. The shells are pink and fawn and speckled like eggs.

'She sells seashells on the seashore,' you say. You sort of sing it out loud and you do it perfect, even though it's very hard to say. If anyone was listening, it would've come out arseways, you're sure. Noel and Cora went to Bray on their honeymoon and she often says she can still smell the seaweedy air that they breathed in every night on the prom. She smiles and looks romantic when she says it, but you think that seaweed stinks and that that is a poor honeymoon memory. But who are you to say? Anyway, the seashell picture is lovely, so at least she has that.

There are pictures of Cora's parents on the mantelpiece and her mother was very fat and had hair that looked like it'd been ironed in bumps across her head. Cora says 'Mother was plain, God bless her,' and you think that Cora didn't pick it off the stones, but you never say that. Cora's father has a jolly face, even if his skin looks like it was boiled. You'd have liked a granda who looked like Cora's father, but your grandas were dead before you got a chance to meet them. Anyway, they were all skinny and sad-looking, like your ma and da. Cora calls her da 'Daddy', like a little kid, and she always says 'Ah, Daddy, the Lord have mercy on him,' but she never says the Lord have mercy on her ma and she calls her 'Mother'. Sometimes you call your ma 'Mother', but only when you're making a point and *only* when she's in a good mood.

Cora's in terrific form and she's singing along to the radio which is turned up very loud. She hasn't a note in her head and you can't hear the songs because of her bad singing, but you let her off in your mind because she's so happy organising the party. And you'll say one thing for her: she knows how to make lovely apple tarts and her custard is never lumpy the way your ma's always is. Your ma makes bananas and custard as a treat sometimes and, apart from the lumps, it's your favourite dessert of all time. You even prefer it to ice cream, which makes your throat gassy. You wouldn't be able to run or skip for long after eating ice cream because you'd have no breath and you'd probably get a collapsed lung. Diluted drinks always give you that tight feeling in your neck as well, like you're nearly choking.

Your ma comes down from your house with trays of sandwiches piled onto the baby's pram. She and Cora do a little dance around the kitchen and you're pink for them, but there's a cinnamon-appley smell and they're in a great mood, so you don't spoil it by being smart-alecky. Your ma lets you sample one of the salmon sandwiches which are cut hotel-style in little triangles. They're yum-yum-pig's-bum so she lets you have one more for luck and you take your time over it. Cora gives you a glass of orange and a Penguin bar and you can't wait to tell Liam because he'll be ripping that he missed all the goodies. Him and the baby are being minded by your auntie Bridget until it's nearly time for the party.

Then you and Cora and your ma blow up balloons until you tingle. Your ma holds up two balloons in front of herself and says 'Hi, I'm Dolly Parton. I'm mighty pleased to meet you', in a fake American accent. Cora nearly chokes with the laughing and you hope your ma doesn't do that later at the party. You give all the glasses a good wipe with a tea towel and leave them on a tray on the sideboard. Your ma hangs up triangle flags on the ceiling – she calls it bunting – and Cora's house is transformed.

'Noel's brother Kit is picking him up and he'll get changed at Kit's house,' Cora says to your ma. 'He thinks we're going to the pictures.'

'Do you need a hand getting dressed?' your ma says, and Cora tells her to get away out of that, she's done enough, and pushes you both out the door. Your ma says cheerio to Cora and the two of you go home to put on your party clothes and get the boys ready. Your ma holds your hand going up the road and you're thrilled.

You wear a blue and white dress that came in a bag from Cora's niece and your ma says it's very flattering. You have new ankle socks and they're gorgeous compared to the knee socks you have for school, which are going grey. Your ma does your hair into two plaits and then she lifts the plaits and clips them across your head. You think you look like a foreigner and you wish you were lovely and tan to go with your new look. Your ma starts calling you Heidi in a silly voice but you warn her not to do that at the party and she stops. Nothing can make her angry today. You stand in front of the mirror in your ma's room and sway this way and that, holding on to the ends of the dress. You're starting to wish it was a maxi, but you decide to be happy with your lot because you're feeling pretty fancy. You turn your head and pat your hair to make sure it's going to stay in place. Your ma pushes you out of the way and says 'Stop titivating', and she puts on her lippy at the mirror. You're proud of her – she's the best looking of all the mothers you know, with her

Kate Bush hair and pale blue eyes and good figure in her clingy brown dress.

Noel's brother is the opposite of him. He's tidy-looking and slim. Kit smokes long cigarettes and you think he's quite handsome. Their other brother, Patsy, is a bit gone in the head. He lives in a home for people that are like him. Kit arrives late to the party with Noel, and even though Cora was ripping before that, she forgives Kit. He brought Noel to the pub and got him sozzled before the party. When they come in, you all shout 'Surprise!' and the baby gets a fright and starts to cry. He's not the only one, because next thing there are tears coming from Noel's eyes. He hugs Cora in front of everyone and swings her back in his arms and kisses her.

'Noel, will you stop?' she says, but everyone can tell that she's delighted. 'That man,' she complains, but her cheeks are red and she's smiling like a mad thing. You all sing 'Happy Birthday' to Noel and he looks like he's going to cry again, so Kit says 'Speech, speech!' and someone else says 'We'll be here all night if that fella starts talking,' and everyone laughs.

You go around with the sandwiches and they all smile at you and say you're a great girl altogether. Kit says you're a smasher and you're delighted with yourself. The food is a big hit and everyone is munching away. Kit can play the guitar and sing, and soon there is a sing-song. Your ma sits on the sofa with her legs crossed, very elegant, drinking beer. Kit is sitting on a kitchen chair across from her.

'Give us a Simon and Garfunkel one,' your ma says.

'A woman after me own heart.' Kit winks at your ma, then he sings the song about silence, which happens to be her favourite. She closes her eyes and sways and sings along, but luckily not too loud.

'You're the life and soul, Kit,' your ma says when he's finished, and she raises her glass to him. Then she drinks it all back in one go and everyone claps and bangs their feet until the last drop has disappeared down her neck. You go into the kitchen and there is no one in there; you try the same thing as your ma with a glass of red lemonade, but the fizz is too much for your nose and it makes your eyes hurt. Then you sneeze twice – watery ones, not thick ones – and you do a loud burp. You can hear Noel and his brother Patsy doing an Elvis song in the sitting room. Noel is actually good, but Patsy hasn't a clue and just makes up the words. You hate the way his face looks and his eyebrows are like two caterpillars crawling across his forehead.

There are chocolate fingers on a plate on the kitchen counter and you scoff loads of them, cramming them into your mouth so fast that you nearly can't swallow them. You wash them down with more lemonade and then you eat one in a dainty way just to show yourself that you can do it. You spread the rest of them around on the plate because they're looking a bit sparse, but you have one more and you savour it by sucking all the chocolate off and letting the biscuit bit melt in your mouth. Then you're sorry you wasted all the other ones; you hardly tasted them, you ate them so fast.

You slip upstairs to the bathroom to look in the mirror and make sure your hair is still alright and that there's no chocolate on your face. Cora and Noel's bathroom is huge; it's like a proper-sized room, not tiny like the one in your house. The door's open so you walk straight in. You get a shock because Kit is in there with his trousers around his ankles, sort of wobbling on his legs and holding himself up over the loo by leaning one hand on the wall. He is holding his thing in his other hand and doing a wee. You can see it clearly and you think that it looks like a droopy flower. You stand and stare at him and he looks into your eyes and then he bends down, swaying a bit, and pulls up his trousers real slow, and all the time he's staring straight at you. You're in a kind of daze and you can't seem to move. Kit smiles at you and blows a kiss with his lips, then he brushes past you and strolls downstairs. When he opens the door at the bottom, the laughing and talking from the party become loud. You just stay standing on the landing outside the bathroom.

Cora waddles up the stairs, huffing and puffing when she gets to the top. 'Are you waiting for the loo, pet?' she asks, and you just shake your head. 'Are you OK?' she says, bending down to look at you and you say that you're grand, even though you feel a bit pale. Cora goes into the bathroom and you don't want to hear her doing her wee – she does it loud like your ma – so you go down to the sitting room.

Kit is sitting on the sofa very close to your ma. You whisper to her that you're going to go home now and that you'll bring the baby. She barely looks at you and just says, 'Grand, grand. Good girl.' She's listening to Kit, who is telling a yarn, and everyone's laughing already even though he's only started it. You are at the front door strapping the baby into his pram when your ma comes out to the hall.

'You wouldn't take Liam as well, would you?' she says, and you say you will and Liam kicks up murder because he wants to stay. He screams that he's going to miss Noel opening his presents and that that's the best bit; then he calls you a bitch and your ma slaps him on the back of the legs for being so bold. He skulks down the road behind you, but you don't care as long as you get home; away from Cora and Noel's. Away from Kit. The baby falls asleep in the pram and you're glad because you need a bit of time to think.

5

Kit

It's a hot morning; the exact kind of day that Noel hates. He always says that the sun's the enemy of the coalman. No one agrees with him, except maybe Cora, because selling coal's their bread and butter. That's what your ma says. On the side of Noel's truck it says: 'The coalman you can recommend to a friend', which is nice and friendly.

You like the sun. Once you got so sunburnt that you had delusions. In bed that night, you thought there were people climbing the walls from the river and coming into your room. They had streams of slimey riverwrack draped all over their bodies and they were humming loudly. They were coming at you from across the room and when you screamed it got stuck in your throat. You felt as though something big and heavy was holding you down on your bed. The sunburn did that to your mind. Your ma said that you'd been struck by the sun. Struck mental, you thought. She put calamine lotion all over your arms and legs and it dried into a pink powder. You still felt hot and itchy and a bit crazy, so she gave you a cool bath. Then she laid you out on towels on your bed and slathered plain yogurt all over you.

'There,' she said. 'You look like a ginormous Golly Bar. Maybe I'll eat you!'

Golly Bars are your favourite ice-pop, but you didn't laugh at what your ma said because you were feeling too loony. After a while the high smell from the yogurt made you vomit all over the place, so she put you back into the bath. It was great the way she minded you. She said afterwards that you'd frightened the shite out of her because your eyes were rolling back in your head and you were babbling a load of nonsense.

On hot days the tar on the road goes into gloopy bubbles that make a 'puh' noise when you break them open with the toe of your sandal. You and Liam get sticks and you poke at the bubbles and pull the sticky black tar around on the road like toffee. But you make sure not to walk in it because the soles of your sandals get stuck. Then they're covered in black gick and the gravel sticks to it and it all becomes a big mess that's impossible to get off. Your sandals feel lumpy under your feet when you walk with all that tar and pebbles stuck to them. Plus it drives your ma crazy because you got tar on the lino before and she couldn't get it off no matter what she did. Even bleach wouldn't shift it.

Sometimes, when you look up the road on a sunny day, you can see a mirage of water floating over the top of the road. It looks like a small lake has floated down from the sky and is content to hover there all day. It's cool; it reminds you of the Sahara desert and gives you a longing to be far, far away. Not that you've ever been to the desert, but you can imagine what it must be like to see a mirage there. But when you're very thirsty, it wouldn't be all that nice.

You and Liam go to the shop early to get milk for the breakfast; you bring him with you. He's still in a bad mood because you made him leave Noel's party early. You put a pair of shorts on him because your ma hates to see him in longers on a nice day; she always says that.

'Sorry about the party,' you say, 'only ma was doing my head in with her singing.'

Liam scuffles along beside you saying nothing. 'Cow,' he says, after a minute.

'Scut.'

'Bitch.'

'Hey, language!' you say and slap him across the head. He gives you a dig back.

'Smelly arse.'

'Sap,' you say and grab his head under your elbow to rub at it with your knuckles. That's called a nuggy.

'La-la-la, the sound of silence, la-la-la,' Liam croaks, doing impressions of your ma and Kit; the two of you have a good laugh.

Mrs Concannon in the shop says some people are in a good mood. That only makes you laugh more because she's a crabby old bag. She says you have the life of Riley, not a care in the world, weeks of doing nothing but pleasing yourselves. Liam sticks out his tongue at her and you have to reef him out of there before she clatters him. You suck Little Devils all the way down the road, showing each other the colour of your tongues. They are your other favourite ice-pop. Liam's tongue is black and you say that that's because he's such a liar. But really Liam's not the worst brother in the world, though he has a snotty nose and he smells piddly a lot of the time.

When you come around the corner, there's a big truck outside Gwen's house. The back of it's open and inside you can see their tall lamp and the hairy brown cushions off their sofa, as well as boxes with things written on them like 'This Way Up' and 'Kitchen Stuff'. The truck means that Gwen's going away forever. It's only now that you realise she'll never sleep in your house again, the two of you awake all night having a chat and a giggle. And she'll never complain when you finally do try to go to sleep that the gushing noise of the weir is keeping her awake. You won't feel her hard, hot body beside you when the dawn starts to creep up the river to your window. And you won't walk to school together again, slagging off everyone, especially Anne with her jelly arse and sunbathed-under-a-sieve freckles and big, sloppy lips.

You drop Liam home and set him up to have his brekky. Then

you let yourself out of the house and go for a walk down to the river bank. Your house is just over the other side of the ivy-covered wall, but it's peaceful, with only the rush of the peat-brown water carrying sticks along with it far away out to the Irish Sea. You sit among the wild garlic on the clabbery bank and let your legs drop over the side towards the water. It's hard to believe that the river has travelled all the way from the Wicklow mountains and through Kildare. You wonder if every little bit of water in front of you has come all that way or if it was created by rain as it went along. You watch the water swirl over rocks and create tiny whirlpools as it streams past.

You have a little cry. Even though Gwen hasn't been around much lately, and you've been fighting a lot, she's still your best friend and you're going to miss her like mad. You watch the two swans who live on the river sail along side by side, so happy together, and that makes you feel worse. You drag yourself up off the river bank and wipe your eyes with the ends of your T-shirt.

When you get home, you try the door of your ma's bedroom, but it's locked. You were hoping to have a chat with her about Gwen going away and who you'd play with now. But she's still tired after the party and you suppose she has a headache, so it's better to leave her alone. You think you hear whispers from behind her door, but you can't be sure. She never talks to herself, she only ever really sings, that's all. She must be talking to the baby, trying to get him to nod off again so she can stay in bed longer.

There's a knock on the front door and it's Gwen. You're glad to see her. She has a big plastic bag in her hand and you can tell that it's filled with books; you can see the bulge of them.

'Here's some books. My mam told me to give them to you. There's some in there for your mam as well.'

'Thank you,' you say and take the bag. You're dying to root through it to see if there's anything good, but you wait your patience. You put the bag down on the floor in the hall. 'So, the truck's here,' you say.

'Yes, we're leaving tomorrow.' Gwen scrapes the toe of her shoe off the ground. Then she jumps at you, gives you a big hug and runs off. She turns to wave and shouts out that she'll write to you. You wave back and then she's gone.

You close the door and lug the bag of books up to your room. You empty them out onto your bed and you're delighted because there are loads of really good ones, like Nancy Drew and Noel Streatfeild. There're a few romantic ones for your ma and you decide to take one of them to see what it's like. You put a book called *Fear of Flying* into the back of your knicker drawer, where no one will see it.

You can hear your ma calling you; she's wondering who was at the door. You tell her it was only Gwen and she asks you to bring her a pot of tea and two cups. You think she must be gasping if she wants a pot, so you make the tea good and strong and then knock on her door. She says just to leave it outside, like a good girl, and go and see where Liam is. You wonder why she's trying to get rid of you, so you just pretend to go out and you stand at the bottom of the stairs and listen. You can definitely hear voices this time and it's not only the baby gurgling to himself in nonsense words or your ma playing with him. There's someone else in there. While you stand staring up the stairwell, the bedroom door opens and Kit comes out wearing just a shirt and underwear. You hear your ma through the open bedroom door, tickling the baby to make him giggle. Kit looks down the stairs; you can't believe what you're seeing. You gawp at him.

'Oh, hello,' he says, grinning his head off like Guy Smiley.

Your eyes tighten and you give him a look, before turning away. You open the front door and slam it hard as you leave so that your ma will know that you know what she's up to.

Liam is playing ball outside and he asks you where you're going. You say it's none of his bloody business. You go over to Cora's house because you've decided to ring your da. The curtains are drawn and there's no answer when you ring the bell. Cora and Noel are obviously still in bed too, the lazy bastards. Your ma has put you in a right mood.

When you get home again, your ma and Kit and Liam and the baby are in the kitchen eating breakfast like one big happy family. The baby's in his high chair as good as gold, not trying to climb out of it onto the table like he usually does. He's feeding himself with a spoon and he's making a grand job of it. Liam's sitting so close to Kit that he's nearly in his lap and he has a big smile glued to his face.

'Look at the puss on this one,' your ma says when you come in.

'Good morning,' says Kit, acting all normal, 'or should I say good afternoon?'

Your ma lets out one of her tinkly laughs that she only does around men.

'What's so funny?' you say to her.

'Oh, get off the stage. We call her Little Miss Prim, Kit. It suits her, doesn't it?'

Kit smiles and says nothing.

'So, Ma,' you say, 'where's Eugene taking you tonight? To a film is it, the same as last week?'

Your ma gives you daggers. 'Go on up now, you, and tidy your room.'

'It's tidy and, anyway, I want my breakfast.'

Kit lights up one of his long cigarettes and you ask does he mind; there are people trying to eat.

'No, I don't mind at all,' he says and takes a drawn-out drag. You could box him in the face for that.

Your ma says that they'll go into the sitting room and leave

Little Miss Prim in peace; they take the baby and their teacups and walk out. Liam follows them like a dog, still chomping on a piece of toast. You take your bowl of Weetabix over to the windowsill and sit down there to watch the river; the windowsill is wide and low, like a seat. There are a couple of canoeists careening down the weir in their long bright boats. You hope that one of them will turn over so that you can count the seconds until he's able to right himself again. You love doing that. The longest you got to count up to before was sixteen seconds and you thought that that canoeist was going to drown. Kit comes back into the kitchen for the ashtray and stops beside you on his way out. He stands there looking out the window and smoking away, but you ignore him.

'Can I help you?' you say after a while, not looking up at him.

'You listen to me, young lady,' he says. 'You'd better behave yourself for your mother, I'm warning you. Don't you ever try to embarrass her like that again.'

'You're not the boss of me; you're not my father,' you say, very quiet. Your face is burning. You don't want to look at him because of his go-through-you eyes.

'That's right; I'm not your father. But you'll do *what* I say, *when* I say it. Do you hear me?'

You get up from the windowsill and stand in front of him. You don't think he's so handsome any more; he's weasely-looking, you think, like a two-legged ferret. He blows the smoke into your face and you push past him into the sitting room where your ma's sitting on the mat at the fireplace, cuddling the baby. She's singing a quiet song into his ear.

'Do you know what, Ma?' you say. She looks up at you with a big smile. She seems so happy, not a bother on her. The baby's snuggling into her arms, ready for his nap. She rubs her hand up and down his chubby little leg. 'Your new boyfriend reminds me of something that you hate,' you say. 'A big, slimy rat!' You shout the last bit and then you run out and up to your own room before she can say anything.

You sit in front of the dressing-table mirror and look at yourself. Your hair's still in two plaits from the night before. You take the hair-bobbins off and comb out the plaits. The hair's all bumpy and you like the way it looks, a bit like your ma's only not as wavy. You think about the look of Kit's thing in his hand in Cora's bathroom at the party. And the way he hooked his eyes on to yours. Your stomach flip-flops. You throw the hairbrush at the mirror and stick your tongue out at yourself. Your cheeks are red.

6

Gwen's gone

You go into town on the bus to meet your da. Liam has a sore throat so your ma keeps him at home and he's going cracked because he likes all the stuff your da always gives you. He says to make sure to bring him back something. He croaks it. You say 'Shut up, froggy, I'll get you nothing,' and he starts crying.

Your ma says not to sit upstairs on the bus and not to talk to any strangers. There's a great view from the top deck; you sit right up the front and pretend that you're driving. You're glad it's not one of the new orange buses. It's one of the cream and black ones, the pint-of-Guinness buses that have an open back door. You love to be so high up looking down on the people waiting at the bus stops, seeing everything going on. There are women talking outside shops before they do their messages, and men out walking fat dogs and crotchety dogs, and kids playing rounders on the greens. You turn around to look at the other people on the bus; they're mostly old. You watch them blessing themselves when they pass a church. You don't bless yourself. Then you feel a bit guilty, so you do it on the sly, scratching your forehead for the in-the-name-of-the-Father bit, then touching your stomach and your shoulders real casual for the next bits.

The bus conductor is gas; he calls you his 'ould segotia', even though you've never met him before. He sings as he goes up and down the stairs collecting the fares and giving out the tickets. You hold your ticket very tight in case the inspector gets on. One time your ma ate her ticket and the inspector got on. When she told him she was after eating it, he said she was disgusting, but he let her stay on the bus.

You think it'll be great – you and your da in town. Maybe you'll do something interesting, like go to the Animal Museum. It's your favourite museum in the whole city. You love looking at the dead insects pinned to cards and the roaring bears that are as stiff as iron in glass cases. But when you get off the bus, your da is standing there hand in hand with Clare, your little half-sister. You always think that Liam has a snotty nose until you see Clare; she has big greeners bunched on her lip all the time and she breathes through her mouth like an old man.

'Howya love?' says your da, kissing you on the cheek. 'Say hello to Clare.'

'Hello Clare.'

'I had to bring her along. Poor Geraldine is throwing up day and night, with being pregnant. She's very bad the whole time, so I said I'd take Her Ladyship out with me to give her a break.'

'Oh.'

Clare looks up at you and does her old man pant. Your da has obviously dressed her; she looks like a farmer in her big woolly jumper and brown cords. At least Geraldine tries to make her look decent, which is a hard job. A bit like Cora and her mother, Clare is plain, God bless her.

'So poor Liam's under the weather,' says your da. 'Ah, he'll be grand in no time, I'm sure. Right, where'll we go so?'

'What about the Animal Museum?'

'Oh, well, the thing is Clare's afraid of the animals in there,' he says, and you can tell it's going to be a brilliant day. 'How's your mammy doing? Alright?'

When you get home, no one answers your knock on the front door, but the back door's open so you let yourself in. You're feeling very important because of the trip into town and home again all by yourself. You call out. You want your ma to see that you got there and back in one piece. And you have to give her the envelope from your da. The house is all quiet and you think they must be in bed having a rest, until you discover that the whole place is empty. You think that's unusual, with Liam being sick and all, but you don't mind; you could do with the silence after a day spent listening to Clare whingeing and breathing like a chain-smoker. She might be your half-sister but that doesn't mean that you have to like her. She kept trying to hold your hand when you went to Stephen's Green to feed the ducks, but you were afraid there'd be snots on her fingers so you pulled away and pointed out a flower or something, to get her away from you. Then she'd start bawling. Your da was moidered with her but he managed to keep his cool. You hope that your da and Geraldine's next child is better than Clare; they could do with a happy, easy baby to make a balance. A baby like your ma's one.

When the baby was in your ma's belly, she thought it was a girl. Everything she had was for a girl, even the names. The baby likes to suck on the clean washing. He crawls over to the plastic wash-basket and grabs wet T-shirts and jumpers and even knickers sometimes, and he pulls them out and puts them in his mouth. He sits there sucking on the clothes, as happy as Larry. Your ma and you used to stop him, but now you let him off.

'He likes the taste of the washing powder, for some reason,' your ma says, 'and what harm will it do him, anyway? It won't kill him.'

You had a little sucky of the washing before, to see, but it tasted like the smell of Daz and you didn't like it. But if the baby thinks it's nice, well, that's OK.

There's still no sign of anyone coming home after an hour and there's only so much reading you can do when your mind is elsewhere, even if it is the juicy bits of *Fear of Flying,* which has turned out to be very good. You have all your favourite pages marked with strips of paper and when you read them, your fanny goes pat-pat-pat and your face gets hot. You only read them in the secrecy of your own room and you make sure that the book is well hidden when you're finished.

They are gone so long that you're worried that your ma might have taken another turn and ended up back in hospital. You wonder if Kit knows that she is a nut job. Maybe he wouldn't call around so much if he knew what she was really like – that she's not all smiles and fake laughs every day of the week. You inspect her room and the bathroom for blobs of blood, but there's no sign of anything strange or startling.

You start to tidy up. Housework is boring but it passes the time. You do all the dishes and you sweep the lino in the kitchen, making sure to do under the table and chairs the way your ma likes. When you've finished that, you wander into the sitting room and hang around by the windows, looking out and hoping to see them coming back. You make yourself a Mi-Wadi, good and strong so that the orangeyness of it makes your throat close in. Maybe Liam had to be rushed to the hospital with his sore throat, you think. Maybe he started vomiting and he choked on it until he was blue, and they're pumping out his stomach with a big tube attached to a machine. You feel sorry for calling him froggy before you left to meet your da.

You decide you'd better go to Cora and Noel's house to see if they know anything. You finish your drink and rush out of the house and you are just heading up the road when you see your ma and the others coming towards you. She is pushing the pram and Liam is trotting along beside her; Kit is with them. His arm is draped over your ma's shoulders and she is looking up at him and laughing. You stop where you are and stare at them coming along. Liam doesn't look very sick. He is licking an ice-pop and kind of skipping after every couple of steps. You sneak backwards before they see you and let yourself into the house. You sit on the windowsill in the kitchen reading an old comic. When they come in, you don't look up until your ma speaks.

'Oh, you're back. How did you get on?' she says.

She lifts the baby out of his pram and kisses him on the forehead. He snuggles his head into her shoulder and his pudgy little arms lie around her neck – right where Kit had his arm a few minutes before. Kit hangs around by the door giving his creepy stare.

'Oh fine, great,' you say and you make a big show of giving her the envelope from your da.

'Oh, thanks,' she says, as if she couldn't care less about the envelope, when normally she is greedy for it, ripping it open to check the amount of money inside. She puts the baby down on the floor, slips the envelope into the food press, and slides the door closed.

Kit says, 'Well, I'll go, so,' and your ma and Liam both tell him to stay. The two of them smiling like a pair of crackpots. You make a snorting noise and, after Kit has left, your ma smacks you across the arm.

'What's that for?' you say, rubbing at the red fingermarks on your skin.

'You know well what it's for, miss,' she snaps, all her smiles gone. She was holding in her bad mood until Kit had gone; you could see it was nearly breaking her face to be nice to him when she was dying to have a go at you.

'I'm sick of him coming around here,' you say.

'Oh, is that right? Well I'm sick of that nosy snot-bag Gwen coming around here, with her thousand-and-one questions, if you must know. "What's that, Mrs Dunne?" "Who's this, Mrs Dunne?" "How's the baby, Mrs Dunne?"'

'Gwen's gone.'

'What do you mean, she's gone?'

'She's gone back to Wales.'

'Well, good riddance, anyway,' says your ma, and she swings the baby onto her hip and puts an angry kiss on his head. She doesn't even say thanks for all the cleaning and tidying you did. And she doesn't ask where you went in town with your da, or what you had to eat.

Sometimes you wish your granny was still alive; when you told her things, her lips moved and she fingered her rosary beads, whether she was holding them or not. But at least she wasn't a mouth like your ma. Your ma has too much to say and you're sick of her. Your granny was quiet; the only noise she made was when she gave you a drop of Lucozade and the orange paper that was around the bottle crackled. Or she'd say a small sentence in a small voice. She never really got angry. If something bothered her, she would say 'Ah well' or 'God is good' or something like that.

You don't like the taste of Lucozade, but you used to drink it for your granny because she was convinced that you loved it. If she was here now, you'd tell her about Kit and she'd probably say 'What will be will be', but not in an annoying way. And she'd give you some of the black chocolate she always ate to keep her regular. You love the sharp-sweet taste of that chocolate she always had. You know that your granny would be sad that none of you were going to Mass any more. Granny loved Mass and had a great devotion to Our Lady. You think Our Lady is morbid-looking with her big pussy face and droopy eyes, but you never said that to your granny.

You sit on the sofa, staring at nothing, thinking about your granny. Your ma comes into the room.

'Look at you, sitting there like a clump of muck,' she says.

'Feck off.'

'Feck off yourself,' she says.

She sits beside you and puts her arm around your shoulder. You shrug her off. She holds you again and this time she gives you a nanny goat's kiss on your cheek with her chin. You half-laugh.

'I'm sorry that Gwen is gone,' she says; 'she was your best friend.' You feel the sting behind your eyes, which means that tears are on the way. 'You're my Little Miss Prim,' says your ma, and you lie back in her arms and she sways you a bit. 'Come on, I got you a Golly Bar; you'd better eat it before Liam gets at it.'

The two of you heave yourselves off the sofa and you go into the kitchen with your arms around each other. Your ma doesn't have many flabby bits but her stomach is soft and it sticks out a little. You have your arm around her waist and you pat her belly with your fingers and feel its squashiness through her clothes. Liam calls it her jelly-belly. She says it's stretched from having babies, including you. You like to think of yourself living under your ma's skin, making it into a tight drum, like the baby used to. It's hard to believe that you were once so tiny that your ma held you in her arms and fed you too. You think it would be perfect to be a baby, not thinking so much about things, and being ferried around in a comfortable pram. That would be the life.

7

THE GREEN MERC

Kit has a surprise for your ma. You're not sure if you want to know about it, but at least it can't be a baby, like your da's surprise, because only women can have babies. Kit's standing at the back door smiling his head off. Your ma's at the sink washing dishes and you're drying. The two of you are having a chat, talking about stuff that's only important to you and her. Kit pulls your ma by the hand towards the door and she asks him what he's at. Her face is pink from standing over the hot sudsy dishwater, and bits of her hair are stuck to her forehead. She scratches her nose and pushes her hair back off her face. Your ma always says that the only time her nose ever gets itchy is when she's up to her neck in washing dishes. Then when she scratches it, the wetness from her fingers makes it worse. That's what happens now. You know, because she looks hot and narked.

Kit drags her by the arm to the door. She pulls off her apron with her free hand and throws it to you. She gives you a what's-this-all-about look. Liam hops up from the table, where he's been making Fuzzy Felt pictures, and follows them out the door. You pick the baby off the floor, nearly tripping over the pots he likes playing with, and carry him on your hip. You don't want Kit to think that you've any interest in his surprise, so you sneak into the sitting room and peep out through the curtains to get a look at what's going on.

He's standing in front of a big car with his hand on the bonnet, looking all delighted with himself. The baby points at the car and says ‘Hah’. Your breath sucks in, despite yourself – the car’s pea-green and it’s beautiful. You decide to go outside. The baby says ‘Hah’ again; he says that about everything.

‘It’s a Merc,’ Liam says to you.

‘I know it’s a Merc,’ you say, giving him a dig. ‘And that’s a Mercedes Benz to you.’

‘That’s exactly right,’ says Kit, patting the car, ‘and isn’t she a beauty?’

‘Who owns it?’ asks your ma.

‘I do!’ says Kit. ‘Well, I half-own her. I own half of her. Noel and myself bought her between us.’

You hate the way he keeps calling the car a ‘her’. It’s stupid. Your ma laughs and he hugs her and lifts her up. She dangles her legs like a little child and she kisses him on the mouth. They make you sick. You’d hate to kiss a man with a moustache like Kit, all hairy and scratchy.

‘Come for a jaunt,’ says Kit.

‘Come where? I can’t just take off,’ she says, ‘I’ve three kids here, you know.’

‘I know that. Bring them!’ he says, smiling at you. An ordinary smile.

You’re thrilled. You hope that everyone you know will see you driving around in a green Mercedes like some kind of princess. Kit is OK sometimes.

‘Oh, I don’t know,’ your ma says, ‘it’s awful late.’

‘Mammy!’ ‘Ah, Ma, please!’ you and Liam say, and she gives in and you all scramble into the car. Kit, your ma and the baby in the front, and you and Liam in the back. It’s gorgeous inside; there are brown leather seats as wide as a field and the backs of your legs get stuck to them. You lift up your legs one at a time and listen to the way they unpeel from the leather with a squelchy sound. There’s an armrest in the middle and you and Liam scrap over it, elbowing each other out of the way. Underneath the smell of Kit's cigarettes there's the rich smell of car: polish, hot plastic and leather. Kit revs up the engine and off you all go.

You head over the bridge, past Gwen's old house which has a 'for sale' sign outside it. The curtains are closed and the grass is getting long in the front garden. Her dad would hate that; he was a big fussy-knickers about their garden. You wave at Gwen's house and shout out 'Goodbye, peasants' like you saw them do in a film one time. Your ma says shut up and not to be making a holy show of her. You see Anne skipping on the corner and you wave at her like a queen, holding your hand flat and turning it. She stops and stares, her mouth hanging in a long gawp, as she watches the car scoot past. Kit beeps the horn and she jumps backwards onto the footpath. You nearly die laughing, but you're not sure if she knew it was you. No one in your area has a car as deadly as the Merc and she probably thinks you're visitors from somewhere posh, like Howth or something.

'So, where are we off to?' your ma asks.

'It's a surprise,' says Kit, 'a magical mystery tour. But we won't go too far today.'

You settle back into the huge seats and enjoy the world going past. You go down a hill, then up a really steep hill. You and Liam are pushed back against the warm leather seats. It's like being on a rollercoaster, you think. Kit says that the Phoenix Park is on the other side of the wall and that it's the biggest walled park in Europe and that the President of Ireland lives there. You think that he's a mine of information and maybe he's not so bad after all.

He points the Mercedes down another hilly road and you see a brown river widening itself away to your left. Kit stops the car and tells you and Liam to look over the wall at the river and to tell him what you see. You see a grey stone house and a low wall; you see shabby windows. You recognise what you see, but it takes you a minute to realise that it's your house and your wall. You can't believe that you are on the other side of the river – it's fantastic! You all stare over at your house for a while and then Kit puts the car in gear and off you go again.

There is a slope full of trees looming over the car and every so often a little house appears from out of nowhere. They are lovely houses, squat and long and painted white; they have narrow flower gardens under their windows and blue doors. They're happy looking houses. Kit says that all the people who live in them used to grow strawberries and sell them and he says that in the olden days there was a ferry across the river to your side. There's still a footbridge but it's closed off. You find it all amazing. The car pulls up at a pub called The Strawberry Hall, which is stuck into the shadowy side of the hill.

'All out!' Kit shouts, but in a nice way.

The inside of the pub is dark and there are mugs hanging from the ceiling. The windows are made of glass squares in red and blue and green. Kit puts you and Liam and the baby at a small table near the door, and him and your ma sit up at the bar. He brings over three glasses and a bottle of red lemonade, and he lets you have the whole lot of it between you.

The smell of the pub is like Cora and Noel's house but the look of it reminds you of your granny's. There's all old stuff on shelves around the place: bottles and pictures and even a pair of clogs. Your granny's shelves were packed with biscuit tins and plates and holy statues. The statues of Holy Mary and Jesus and Saint Philomena were nearly knocking each other off the shelves, there were so many of them. Your granny loved Our Lady, and people were always bringing her back plastic Marys and fonts and miraculous medals from Knock, Fatima and Medjugorje. She always wanted to go to Lourdes but just when she was finally going to get her wish, she died. The priest at her funeral said that it was a shame and a pity that someone so holy should miss out on such a sensational pilgrimage. Your ma snorted when he said that and did a little laugh.

'It's an even bigger shame that she beat her kids senseless when she was drunk,' she said, real loud, to your auntie.

Your auntie didn't take kindly to that; she was very sad that your granny was dead – she was crying. Your auntie is called Bridget after the most famous woman-saint in Ireland. All your granny's children are named for saints: Saint Joan of Arc, Saint Bridget of Kildare, Saint Anthony of Padua and Saint Francis of Assisi. You know all their names because your granny made you say them with the places they were from. She liked saints. Your auntie Bridget is Big Miss Prim, the way you are Little Miss Prim. She is your cousin Rory's mother, but she is not a virgin or a saint because they are people who've never had sex and sex is what makes babies. That's what Gwen told you, anyway.

Noel says that Bridget is like something that fell off a Christmas tree because she wears baubly earrings and loads of make-up, even in the morning time. All her clothes are the same colour: purple. She wears different kinds of purples: mauve, indigo, aubergine, lilac, maroon, lavender. She always dresses up. Your auntie's good to herself; she has a footstool to put her feet up on and a woolly blanket for her legs when it's chilly. She gets out of bed around ten o'clock in the morning and she doesn't do the shopping because she hates supermarkets. Your ma says that her husband and Rory should be canonised for putting up with her. Your auntie Bridget looks down her nose at your ma because her and your da don't live together any more. She doesn't visit your house much and when she does, she passes remarks on the furniture and the food and the cleanliness of things.

After your granny's funeral you all went to a pub for drinks and food, and the sambos were stale on the edges. Your auntie went mental at the barman because she had paid for the sandwiches and all, and she expected a decent spread to send her mother off with. The barman got the manager and he told your auntie to get a grip and she flung her drink into his face. Then you all had to leave. You never even got to have a cocktail sausage and there were tons of them in baskets and you love them. You always wonder who ate them in the end.

In The Strawberry Hall your ma has a snowball, which is a very fancy drink, and Kit has a pint of cider. They are making jokes with the man behind the bar and he laughs and wipes glasses and serves drinks, all at the same time. You're glad that you're sitting far away from them at a table by yourselves, because you can pretend you're not with them. And you don't have to be looking at him putting his arm around her waist and kissing her neck and running his paws through her hair. She doesn't seem to mind it, but you do. You think it would be better if Kit would feck off back to wherever he came from, Merc or no Merc. The baby is giddy. He keeps waddling over to the door and pointing out to the road with his sausagey little arm. You are fed up hopping up and down after him; he won't stay still. Liam is happy slurping his lemonade and staring at the other people in the bar.

The next thing you know, Kit says, 'Why don't we all take our drinks outside?' and you cross the road to sit beside the river. Your ma and Kit lie beside each other on the riverbank. They are whispering and laughing and he keeps grabbing at her. You sit and stare at them, hoping they'll stop, which eventually they do. They sit up and drink their drinks. There's a family near you having a picnic on a blanket. The da has big buck teeth and Kit says 'The state of Bugs Bunny' and 'What's up doc?' and your ma laughs very loud. She is drinking a lot of snowballs and then she changes to Babycham, which is sparkly and the colour of watery pee. Kit goes over the road and back to the pub to get the drinks.

It's such a nice evening. The sun creeps in and out from behind low clouds, making fast shadows on the trees and the river. The family with the picnic are eating lettuce and tomatoes and shiny slices of ham off blue plastic plates. You can't take your eyes off the picnic family. They have a flask of tea and they take turns sipping from the cup that screws off the top of the flask. The ma calls herself a silly billy because she forgot the rest of the cups. They talk a lot to each other and you can see the bits of food in their mouths and stuck to their teeth. The ma and the kids keep on laughing at what the da says and you think he's goofy looking, but they all seem to think he's great.

Kit lights up a cigarette and you do some loud tuts and he tells you to take your brothers off for a little walk. You don't want to but your ma gives you a look, so you pick up the baby and bring the two of them a bit of the way down the riverbank. It's funny to be on the wrong side of the river. The bank is low and the water beside you is shallow and yellow-coloured instead of brown. And it's flowing the wrong way.

You wonder if the picnic family know that the green Merc belongs to you. You go over and stand beside it, just in case they don't. Soon the others join you and you all get back into the car. You glance at the picnic family to make sure they're watching, but the buggers don't even seem to have noticed you. Kit starts singing as you drive along and Liam and your ma join in. He sings a song that goes:

One man went to mow, went to mow a meadow,

One man and his dog, Spot, went to mow a meadow.

Then he adds bits like:

One man and his dog, Spot, a bottle of pop, went to mow a meadow.

And he keeps adding on more things until the man has loads of stuff with him in the meadow, which is what they call a field in England. It's very good but you don't give Kit the satisfaction of singing along in the car; you practise it at home so that you remember all the words. Liam and your ma are like two saddos shouting the song and mumbling the bits they forget. Even the baby loves it.

8

A Fight

You're clumsy. You're always letting things drop and knocking them over. Sometimes your hands just don't do what you expect them to do. Sometimes a thing will seem to move by itself, as if it has life inside it, when it's only a table or a jug or a can on a shelf. Your ma says you're like a bull in a china shop and you hate being called that; bulls are bulky and ugly. And they are men, which you're not.

Your ma won't let you touch anything if you go shopping with her and she gets hyper if she sees your hand reaching for something, to see what it feels like. 'Put that down, put that down, put that down,' she says, when your hand is hovering and you haven't picked anything up. She says it loads more times if you *do* have something in your hand and she sees it. Even if you hold it for a second and it's only something like a jar of carrots or a bottle of minerals. She's terrified that you'll drop it and make a mess and that she'll have to pay for it. You wouldn't really mind if you dropped something in a shop by accident. It'd be great to see that jar of little frilly carrot slices smashed all over the floor, sliding under the shelves of food like lost goldfish. You wonder if those jar-carrots are soft and squishy or if the ridges on them make them hard. Your ma only ever buys the ordinary carrots that have dirt on them and grassy stalks and that have to be peeled and sliced before you can eat them.

Sometimes you bash into things. You don't do it on purpose; it just happens. It's like as if your eyes don't see things quick enough; or, if they do, that your body disobeys your eyes. Sometimes you think things must move by themselves because there's no way you were going to knock into something and then wham! you have bruises on your legs and the tops of your arms. You've had one of the bruises for ages and ages. It's on your hip and you get it because you're always banging into the corner of the kitchen table, on the exact same spot. That bruise goes from navy blue to green to yellow and back to navy again; fresh bruise on top of old. The middle of it hurts when you press it with your finger. You don't show that bruise to your ma. She sees the ones on your legs when you wear a dress and she always says the same thing: 'Jesus, Mary and Joseph, what happened to your legs?' Then she pulls at your skin, pinching it between her fingers while she tries to get a better look. That nearly hurts more than the bruises because, unless you poke at them, their soreness doesn't last. You tell her to get off you. She thinks she owns you the way she goes on.

Anyway, mostly you wear longers and they hide your legs. Your ma likes to see Liam in shorts on a warm day, but she doesn't mind about you. She doesn't make you wear skirts or dresses if you don't want to.

Gwen's mother always told her what to wear. She used to say that you looked like a pair of tomboys going around; she preferred Gwen to wear a skirt. You like being called a tomboy – it singles you out – and you think maybe you might get your hair cut short to look like Huckleberry Finn, but you like your long hair, even if it is ratty-looking. And you like dresses too. What you'd really love is a pair of jeans, but you don't ask your ma for them anymore, because the last time you asked she said jeans are for binmen and that's all they're suitable for. She wears a denim skirt which is made from jeans material, but when you pointed that out, she said 'That's different.' She looks real cool when she has that skirt on, especially when her legs are a bit tan and she puts on her brown sandals. You're proud of how nice-looking your ma is but you'd also like it if she wasn't sad and narky all the time. Then she'd be perfect.

Kit works in a butcher's shop. You found that out from Cora, who is always gabbing. Cora says that Kit is a bit of a catch; that single men of his age are few and far between. Your ma says 'He's not exactly ancient,' and Cora says 'Beggars can't be choosers.' Your ma asks her what that's supposed to mean but Cora doesn't answer.

You can imagine Kit behind the counter in the butcher's, up to his neck in blood and guts, hacking away at lumps of pig and cow and lamb. He'd be touching all the disgusting things like livers and wodgy bits of pudding and worse things, like ox hearts.

You see him in your head, wearing a stained apron, smiling at all the ladies while he wraps slabs of meat, soggy with blood, in that soft paper. His feet are in wellies and there's a load of sawdust stuck to them, like an extra pair of shoes. It suits him, you think. He looks like the type of person who *should* spend their day chopping up animals, blood splattered all over himself.

Now you know why he brings bags of sausages and rashers to your ma as presents. You couldn't believe it when he first arrived with them. At first, you refused to eat any in case they were poisoned, but the smell of the rashers frying was so gorgeous that you gave in after a while and ate some. They were lovely; hardly any fat.

'Eugene used to bring her flowers,' you say to Kit.

'Well, I'm not Eugene, am I?' he says, real smart. 'And anyway, flowers won't feed a growing family.'

'We don't need you to feed us.'

'I don't hear anyone else complaining.'

You could whack him in the shins for that. He's always trying to pick fights with you and your ma never takes your side.

'Now, now, you two,' she says, as if Kit is her child too. He acts like one anyway.

You're all having your tea, Kit included. He's going on about the car, as usual, trying to think of a name for it.

'What about calling her Stella?' he says, sipping his tea.

'Nah,' your ma says. 'What about Nora?'

'No. Nora is too boring – it sounds like a nurse or a teacher or something. It needs to be a catchy name, something fast.'

'Mercedes is a girl's name already, isn't it? It's Spanish, as far as I know. Just call the car Mercedes.'

Kit rolls his eyes. Even you think that's a thick suggestion. 'Maybe I'll call her Tallulah.'

You nearly choke on the milk you're drinking. 'Tallulah? What kind of a name is *that*?' you say. 'Anyway, why does it have to be a woman's name?'

'I know,' pipes up Liam. 'Call the car Joan, after Mammy.'

Kit rubs him on the head and says that that's a brilliant suggestion, but there's only room for one beauty called Joan in his life. You make puking noises and your ma laughs. You get up to leave them to it and, by accident, you knock Kit's mug of tea into his lap. You can see it happening nearly before it does, and you grab at it to try to stop it, but the mug flies off the table and tips the scalding tea all over him. Kit jumps out of his chair, swiping at his wet trousers, and the mug falls to the floor and smashes.

'You stupid little bitch,' he shouts, right into your face.

The room goes quiet. Your ma stands up. She puts her hands on the table and leans her whole body forward; her lips have disappeared. Everything stops. You all stand and stare at each other, your eyes bugging out of their sockets. Your ma drops her head and points to the door.

'Get out,' she whispers, not looking up.

You don't move, you feel like your sandals are stuck to the lino as if it was made of gooey tar. It takes you a few seconds to realise that your ma's not talking to you. Liam and the baby both start to cry.

'Ah Joan,' says Kit, but then he goes to the door and walks out.

Liam is hiccupping, squeezing fat tears out of his eyes. The baby is rubbing at his hair and looking at your ma.

'Stop that nonsense,' your ma snaps at Liam and he holds his breath. Then all the hiccups get backed up in his throat and his nose starts snuffling snots out of it like a waterfall. His face is getting redder and redder and the snots are going in and out of his nose with the breaths he's holding in. 'Jesus, Mary and Joseph, will you get a hanky and tidy yourself up!' she roars. 'And you! Clean up that mess.'

You wipe the table and clear up the broken mug and spilled tea from the floor. Your ma sits into the windowsill and stares out at the river, not moving or saying a thing. You do an extra special tidy up around the kitchen, but she doesn't move, even when you say you're finished. The baby is quiet, watching your ma from his highchair; you lift him out and take him into the sitting room to play so that he won't bother her. When you go back in a while later to get some juice for his bottle, she's still sitting there, looking at the river, watching it swirl by.

The baby has a box of books, little books with hard cardboard pages that are all curled up on the edges because he likes to suck them. He looks at the pictures of the baby animals in the books: foals and calves and kittens and puppies. The animals remind you of him because they are tiny and have to be minded well. He puts the little books in and out of the box and chats to himself, very busy. You sit beside him on the floor and watch him.

You like holding the baby when he's tired. His body gets warm and heavy with sleepiness and his eyes look soft. His hair is extra fluffy on the back of his head from where he lies on it at night. When he's tired of playing, he lolls back in your arms and cuddles his face into your belly. You pop his soother into his mouth and rock him this way and that until he falls asleep. Then you bring him up to your ma's bed and lie beside him, until he settles there.

When you get back down to the kitchen, your ma is at the table with a bottle of beer and a glass. It's nearly dark and she has the bad mood face that you haven't seen in a while.

'Will I turn on the light for you?' She doesn't answer but you decide not to turn it on in case she shouts. 'I'll leave you so,' you say then.

'Why does it always happen to me?' she says, very quietly.

You haven't a clue what she means and, really, you'd prefer to be up in your room reading *Fear of Flying* or having a go of the Sindy dolls. But you know she'll kill you if you try to escape.

'Is it the broken mug?' you ask.

She sniggers through her nose, a short, dry noise that isn't really a laugh at all. 'More like the broken men.'

'Oh,' is all you can think of to say.

You wonder if she's going to end up back in Saint Angela's. You hope not because then Cora and Noel will be staying, hawing smoke into your face and nosing around the place. It's not so bad when you have school to go to and can get away from them, but it would be the pits to have to spend the whole of your summer holidays with them.

'Go on up to b-e-d,' she says, spelling it out as if your brothers were still in the room.

'Y-e-s,' you answer. She smiles, takes a gulp of her beer, and waves you out the kitchen door.

You check on the baby and Liam, who are both in the land of nod, thank God, and then you go into your own room and look around. Nothing is interesting to you. You find that you can't read and the Sindys only bore you with their nonsense. You do what your ma was doing and stare out the window at the river, at the way it knots and turns in the dark below the window.

You're kind of glad that you knocked the tea into Kit's lap, in a way. You didn't do it on purpose but at least it got rid of him and it seems that your ma might be glad too. She said he was broken. At least you think that's what she said. She seems a bit sad, but really she's probably delighted to see the back of him because he is such a bossy-boots and a show-off and a know-it-all. Compared to Kit, Noel is saint-style and you'd prefer him any day of the week, manky fingernails and all. You hope that Noel hasn't got any more brothers up his sleeve, apart from slow Patsy, because that's all you'd need.

You stay looking out at the river, listening to it swish on past the house until your eyes beg for sleep. You were hoping to hear your ma come up, hoping that she might only have the one drink and then pop off to bed, but there's no sign of her. You go and lie on the bed in your clothes and bury your face into the smell of yourself on the pillow. You're too tired to get undressed, so you pull the eiderdown over you to keep warm. You're just drifting off when the door opens. It's Liam.

'Can I come in with you?'

'Have you wet your own bed?'

He shakes his head, so you nod and he tuckles in beside you, his back to your front. You put your arm around him and snuggle your nose into the warm back of his neck.

'Night, night,' he mumbles and you whisper the same thing back.

9

The New Baby

Anne calls to your door and asks if you want to come out to play. She has her skipping rope with her. It has wooden handles that are painted red and blue, and the rope part is white and thick. Skipping's all the rage. It used to be hopscotch – you could draw the best grid – but that's ancient history now. You don't have a proper skipping rope. You tie a bit of washing-line to the handle on the front door and you bribe Liam to turn it for you. You give him a few coppers, or sometimes you say you'll dry the dishes when it's his turn. You practise running into the rope while he turns it. You're getting really good at it and it makes you feel light when you do it properly.

'Skipping is for saps,' you say to Anne.

'Well, we don't have to play skipping; you can come around to my house if you like.'

You've only ever been in Anne's house once. They have a leather sofa, like the seats in Kit's green Merc, only bigger. They have supper in Anne's house, tea and toast with butter, very late. Gwen told you that before. You say 'OK', as if you couldn't care less, but really you're dying to go to her house because they're rich and they have a Soda Stream that makes drinks and everything.

Anne's ma has blonde hair. She always looks well – the same way your auntie Bridget does – with loads of make-up all the time. Your ma says she's a bottle blonde, which means her hair is not real. Anne's ma is a hairdresser and she runs her own place. Cora might be going there to work. Your ma says she'd rather pull her toenails out with a pliers than work for that wagon, but Cora says she's bored hanging around the house all day.

'It's well for some who have the luxury of boredom,' your ma says, real snotty.

'It's well for those who have kids to keep them busy,' Cora says, and then her face rumples and she starts to cry and there are snots sliding out of her nose. You and your ma nearly die.

'Here, you're welcome to take this lot any day; I'll just go and pack their bags,' she says and you both laugh. Cora just sniffs and smiles a little.

Anne's ma's hair salon is called Krazy Kutz. It's spelled wrong on purpose, to make it more jazzy. You wonder what Cora could do there with her claw hands, but your ma says you'd be surprised; Cora is very deft despite her handicap.

You go to Anne's house and her ma gives you a Cola Soda Stream and fairy cakes with pink icing. Only one each. You think it's amazing that Anne is so fat when her ma only gives you one tiny cake at a time. It's even more amazing that Anne is so brilliant at Irish dancing. You call her ma Mrs Brabazon or Mrs B, but her name is Margaret. Anne's da calls her Mags. You wonder why Mrs Brabazon married someone so ugly-looking, when she's so pretty herself. Anne is kind of piggy-looking, like her Da, who has bright red hair and squidged-up eyes. Mrs Brabazon says that Anne is pleasantly plump, but that just means fat. Your ma says that Mags was obviously after Mr Brabazon's fat wallet, not his fat arse.

'Now, ladies,' Mrs B says, 'I'll love you and leave you. Cheerio!'

She always talks like that. Anne talks a bit funny too sometimes, because she goes to elocution, which is a place where they teach kids how to say poems in posh voices. She won a prize for reciting 'Rainy Nights' by Irene Thompson, which made you jealous because that's your favourite poem. When her ma's gone, you have the house to yourselves. Anne shows you her Irish dancing medals;

the whole room is stuffed with them. You have no medals for anything. She brings you up to Mrs B's room to look through her stuff. There are loads of different jars of creams and powder and everything smells lovely. You and Anne try on some perfume – you have to squeeze a tassled bulb to make it come out – and then you sneeze over and over. They are big meaty sneezes and you have no hanky and a glob of snot gets stuck to your hand. You wipe it off on the underneath of the dressing table when Anne isn't looking.

Their whole house smells sweet, not like your house, which smells like the river sometimes: thick and damp and wet. They have a woman who comes in to clean for them. You think it would be great if your ma had someone who could come in and help her with all the cleaning and washing and cooking. Your ma can't stand housework, so she gets you and Liam to help out. Mostly you hate it, but sometimes you don't mind it; you can even be in the mood for it. But it's impossible to keep the place clean when the baby mushes biscuits and yogurt into everything.

Anne says that her da sleeps in the spare room and she shows it to you. It's smelly, like farts, and there are trousers and shirts all over the floor. The blankets are falling off the bed.

'He's in her bad books at the moment,' Anne says, while the two of you stand at the door staring in.

'Why?'

'Gwen's mam,' she says but you don't know what she's on about.

'They're gone back to Wales.'

'And it's just as well,' Anne says, closing the door, which is a relief because the smell is making you feel sick.

You go down to the kitchen which is huge like a room off the telly. Anne goes to the press and gets out more cakes and you have two each. They're so lovely – shop-bought with pale sponge and slippy white cream. The two of you eat them so fast, you end up with bits of icing and creamy stuff all around your mouths. You watch Anne poking her tongue at the sides of her mouth, trying to lick it all off. She has freckles the size of ha'pennies and you're glad that you don't have any of them. You have beauty spots but Anne says that they're really called moles. You say that moles are a type of animal and she says that you're wrong – that the animals are called voles.

'Voles,' you say. 'That's stupid.'

'You're stupid!'

'You're fat!' you say, and storm out of the house. You feel a bit bad though once you're outside, so you ring the bell and say you're sorry and she lets you back in. The two of you watch telly, but there's nothing good on, so you say why don't you go out the back and take turns with her skipping rope.

When you get home, your ma corners you at the back door.

'I've a bone to pick with you,' she says.

'What?' you say, shoving past her into the kitchen.

'Hold on there, young lady.' She grabs your collar and manages to pull the short hairs at the back of your neck.

'Ow!' you scream, exaggerating a bit, just to let her know that she's hurt you. She pushes you on to a chair and sits down opposite you at the table.

'Did you tell Liam that Geraldine and your father are having a new baby and that your da's especially hoping for a boy?'

'I might have.'

She sighs. 'Did you or didn't you?'

'I might have said about the baby coming but I didn't say anything about them wanting a boy.'

'Well, Liam's been crying all morning in his room because somehow he thinks your father is going to replace him with a *new* boy baby.' She stares into your eyes. 'Well?'

'Well what?'

She swipes at you but you duck. 'You watch your tongue, missy,' she says. 'I specifically asked you not to say anything to Liam. You know how badly he takes things. Now he says he never wants to see your father again and you're both supposed to be meeting him next week.'

You did tell Liam about the baby. He kept wanting to hang around with you and Anne; she is bad enough by herself without having to deal with Liam too.

'I'm sure Liam doesn't mind if he never sees da again,' you say.

'Watch it,' she snaps. 'Well, you can think about what you've done while you're minding him and the baby. They're upstairs. I'm going down to see Cora and I won't be back for a couple of hours.'

'But –'

'Don't but me, young lady. You'll take care of your brothers and you'll be good to Liam. You hurt his feelings, and if you can't see that, you're even worse than I thought.'

She swings out through the door. You're fed up with the way she bosses you around. You're more like a slave than a daughter and it's obvious that she hates you, and that she cares more about the boys and bloody Cora and Noel than you. And probably Kit as well, even though she's fighting with him at the moment. She might have taken your side against him, but you bet she's regretting it now. She's probably gone to Cora's house hoping that he'll be visiting Noel and that she will conveniently bump into him. You bet that's what she's up to.

Sometimes you wish that your ma was dead and that you, Liam and the baby lived in an orphanage. The people in the orphanage would feel really sorry for you and they would sing songs to you and let you sit on their laps. They'd bring you on picnics in meadows and they'd have a big basket, a chequered blanket and a flask and stuff. Then one day a rich couple would come and adopt the three of you and you would all live happily ever after in a big old house with ponies to ride on.

The adoption ma would be movie-style pretty and the adoption da would be tall and handsome and he'd wear a suit and tie. Your da never wears a suit because he's an electrician and he wears jeans or cords and jumpers. You like to think about all that sometimes, but the good feeling of it doesn't last because the guilt starts creeping up your body and into your mind. It's not right to wish that people are dead, especially not a close relative, even if they are narky all the time and make your life a living hell. Your ma has her good points; she just doesn't like to show them very often.

It starts to rain and you can hear the fat drops banging off the windows. You stand at the back door and look out into the scrubbiness of the yard. It's warm outside and the rain creates a hot smell in the air, like blown-out matches. You have no garden, only a concrete back yard with weeds pushing up everywhere. It's dirty because the bags of coal and slack that Noel delivers in his truck have left their black powder everywhere and lumps of coal are spilled all around. The rain mixes with the coal powder and makes small black rivers across the yard.

Upstairs you can hear your brothers scuttling in the bedroom, laughing and throwing toys around; they're probably playing with their cars. The baby doesn't really know how to play properly and Liam gets angry with him for messing up the game, but they seem to be having fun. You're glad, because you feel sorry for what you said to Liam about your da's new baby. You didn't think it would make him so sad.

You cook some beans on toast for the three of you to have for your tea and you call them down. The baby loves beans and he picks them up with his fingers, which he shapes into little lobster claws; he pops the beans into his mouth, one by one. Liam sits there with a big puss on him.

'Cheer up, Mr Grumpy,' you say and he humphs at you. But there's a smile at the corners of his mouth. 'Humpy Grumpy

Dunne, that's your new name.'

'Feck off, smelly arse,' Liam says, shoving a huge spoonful of beans into his mouth, and you know that he forgives you because at least he's slagging you.

His eye-rims are all red from crying. They're the colour of peeled tomatoes, a sort of sludge red. You grab his head under your elbow and give him a nuggy, making sure not to hurt him or pull his hair. He starts laughing and so does the baby. The baby's new laugh is false; he crinkles up his eyes and peeps out of them and pretends to laugh. It's very funny and it sends you and Liam into convulsions. He's such a clever baby; probably the cleverest one in Ireland.

Outside the window a jackdaw squawks in the rain; giving out, probably, because his feathers are getting wet. Jackdaws seem to gather around your house; they have shiny bellies and are always complaining. A bit like a lot of the people you know. Liam starts to make jackdaw noises and waves his arms up and down like wings. The baby chuckles and sniggers – real laughs this time. You look at your brothers and you're glad that you are you, and that you're not in some orphanage which would probably be horrible anyway, like the ones in the films.

10

A Letter

You get a letter from Gwen. It's on purple fancy paper and it has a strong smell which your ma says is violets. They're obviously the type of flower that smell kind of lovely and horrible at the same time. Gwen doesn't have much to say in the letter. She is not homesick for Dublin. She loves Wales and she even has a new friend called Olive, but she says that you are still her best friend forever. You think Olive is a weird name, kind of ancient and long-sounding; it would suit an old granny.

You wish Gwen was back, she had a bit of life in her, not like Anne, who never wants to do anything interesting. All Anne feels like doing is lazing in her room, yapping on about boys and the women who work in her mother's hairdressers, and you're expected to sit and listen. You prefer to be outside, hanging around or whatever. She's not even allowed down near the river – her da won't let her; he says it's a deadly dangerous spot. Anne doesn't like coming to your house. Sometimes she says she just doesn't want to and other times she tells you she's not allowed. Her place is great because there are always loads of goodies to have, but you're fed up spending the bright warm days in the dark of her house, doing nothing.

You tell Anne about the letter from Gwen.

'So?' she says, about Gwen's letter, but then she gets you to read it out to her. Her face goes all red under her freckles and she does a cutting laugh when you finish reading. You don't bother to tell her about all the hugs and kisses that Gwen put on the end; they nearly fill the bottom half of the page. That would probably send her over the edge. 'Gwen's a wagon,' she says.

You fiddle with your hair. 'No she's not.'

'Well, her mam is anyway.'

You can't be bothered listening to Anne and the way she goes on, so you go home. Your ma's sitting at the kitchen table and you're amazed to see that Kit's there too, walking up and down in front of the window. They're talking and don't notice you at first. You do a big 'Ahem' and they stop and look at you.

'Oh, hello there,' he says.

'Go on back out now,' your ma says. 'Kit and myself are talking.'

'So I see,' you say, marching through the kitchen. You plod up the stairs to your room making huge noises with your feet on each step. It's not one bit funny the way Kit has wormed his way back in your ma's door. You were sure he was gone forever but there he is, sliming around and licking up to her again. It makes you sick.

You start a letter to Gwen on your best paper. It has a picture of a pink rose faded into it, but there's no smell. It has envelopes to match and it was a present from your ma. She gave it to you for nothing; it wasn't your birthday or Christmas or anything.

Every Girl's Handbook says that the name Gwen means white, which can't be right because Gwen has black hair. But it would suit Anne. The handbook says that Anne means 'God has favoured me', but how can a name mean something like that? You were going to tell Gwen what her name means in the letter, but now you're not sure. Your name is not in the book, which is typical, and it's the whole problem with having an Irish name – nobody cares about them. *Every Girl's Handbook* was printed in Italy but made in England, in Middlesex. Middle sex. Sex is what makes babies; Gwen told you that, but you already knew.

It's hard to know what to say in the letter. You don't tell her about Kit; nothing about him. You say you're hanging around with

Anne, but only because you have to; there's no one else to play with. You make everything sound very boring on purpose, so that Gwen will know that nothing has changed. Then you think that maybe you should make up some exciting stuff, but you don't want to waste too much paper, so you don't bother.

You tell Gwen that the baby is bigger, that he can say 'Yeah' now and that it doesn't matter what you ask him – that's what he answers. You could say to him 'Are you an alligator?' or 'Did you just drop out of the sky?' or 'Would you like a bun?' and the baby says 'Yeah'. You let her know that your ma is not mad any more, that she's in great form altogether, and that Liam's as full of snots as ever. You tell her that your uncle in Washington has recovered from the volcano, but you scribble over that bit in the end.

There's a lot of noise coming from downstairs. You can hear shouting, so you tiptoe out onto the landing to hear better. Noel is down there, cursing and roaring about something. You go down the stairs dead quiet, and listen outside the kitchen door.

'What the hell is your problem, Kit?' shouts Noel.

'I've no problem, Noel. What's *your* problem?' Kit says this real calm. You can nearly feel the heat from Noel through the door; you know that when he's annoyed, he goes deep red and he puffs through his nose.

'You're a bloody little pup,' Noel says. 'Patsy has more sense than you.'

'Ah, get a grip; you can't tell me what to do any more. This is between Joan and me. It's none of your fucking business.'

'It *is* my business when those kids are involved.'

Your ma isn't saying anything. She's probably delighted in one way that Noel's standing up for her, but in another way she's probably dying to kiss the face off Kit and forget about everything that happened before. That's typical of her. There's no point in hanging around to listen, anyway.

You go down to see if Cora's in, to get away from the shouting and the noise. She might have a stamp that you can use to send your letter to Gwen. Cora's very organised and her house is full of useful things like stamps. Your ma says it's because she has feck all else on her mind, but it never stops her from borrowing things like scissors or a measuring tape from Cora when she needs to.

'Hello, pet,' Cora says when she sees you at her door, 'come on in and have a glass of lemonade.'

Cora has a cup of tea and a fag while you sip your fizzy drink. You pretend not to mind her blowing the smoke all over you; it's her house and she can puff away if she wants to.

'Cora, is there any such animal as a vole?' you ask.

'No, not at all; but there's definitely one called a mole. I don't think we have any moles in Ireland; they mustn't be fond of rain.'

She puts the hand with the cigarette close to her mouth and pulls hard on it. Cora's hands are fascinating the way they curl in on themselves. You knew you were right about the mole. That Anne's a big thick. You can't wait to set her straight. Cora's from down the country and she knows everything about animals and farms and all that kind of thing.

'Noel is around at our house.'

'Oh,' she says, not looking at you, and you know that she knows that Noel has gone to yours to have a word with Kit. Cora says that your ma deserves better than that Kit fella, that he's a blackguard and a consequence. She *used* to say he was a good catch but not anymore. You heard them talking about Kit before, and Cora said to your ma that he was a fly-by-night and that she should watch herself. Your ma got annoyed with Cora in a quiet way. You knew by her face that she thought that Cora was trying to put a dampener on everything and get in the way of her fun.

'He's not the worst,' she said.

'Ah, no, I know that Joan, but you're not the first, let me put it that way.'

'I'd be an eejit if I thought I was the first, Cora.'

'I mean, you're not the first *separated* woman he's been with.'

Cora said '*separated*' slowly, as if your ma was a bit stupid. Her lips nearly disappeared when Cora said that. Your ma hates being called 'separated'.

'Anyway, it's not as if I want to marry him.'

Cora said it was just as well and then they both stared at you and stopped talking altogether.

The door bangs open and Noel barges in. 'Jesus effing Christ,' he shouts, 'there's a bloody pair of them in it. A pair of dopes!' Then he sees you and he goes 'Oh' and he asks Cora for a cup of tea and says he'll be in the sitting room.

'Don't mind Noel and the language,' she says.

'It's all the same to me.'

Cora gets Noel's tea ready and she butters biscuits and puts them on a plate. 'He's a divil for the buttered Mariettas,' she says. You're mad for them yourself; you love squishing two together and watching the butter ooze out through the holes, like tiny yellow worms. 'Have a couple there, pet.'

'Thanks, Cora,' you say, thinking she's a good neighbour and a nice friend for your ma. At least she's not flighty like the way Gwen's mam was, always going to parties and wobbling around in high heels.

'I believe Bridget's boy is going to be staying in your house,' Cora says, when she comes back from giving Noel his tea and bickies.

'How do you mean?'

'Oh, maybe I wasn't supposed to let on. Young Rory, he's coming to your house for a while, isn't he?' She lights a cigarette and sucks in a big gasp of smoke.

You make a moany noise. 'Why does *he* have to come?' you say.

'Well, between me, you and the wall, himself and his father are not seeing eye to eye these days. And your auntie Bridget thinks it would be better for everyone if Rory was away from the house for a while.'

'Why can't Uncle Jack be the one to go away? Then Rory could stay where he is.'

'Ah, well, it's not as easy as that, is it?'

The next thing Kit arrives into Cora's kitchen. He doesn't even knock, just waltzes in.

You jump up. 'I have to go.'

'Don't leave on my account,' he says, twiddling his stupid moustache and doing one of those half-smiles. 'Make us a cup of tea there, Cora.'

'Don't flatter yourself; she was leaving anyway, weren't you, pet?' Cora smiles and you nod and let yourself out.

You can't believe that your ma never told you that your cousin was going to be living at your house. You need that like a hole in the head. You ask her about it when you get home. She is scrubbing the kitchen floor, which is her least favourite job on earth, and she's doing a great job of it. She doesn't say anything about Kit, or what he said, or what she said to him. So you don't mention it either. The kitchen smells like smoke and lemons. Her face is red – she has grog blossom cheeks from the basin of water and the scrubbing.

'Is Rory coming to stay with us?' She stops working and looks up at you.

'Oh, I was going to tell you. You don't mind do you? He'll share Liam's room. You won't be put out.'

'Can you not tell Auntie Bridget that you've changed your mind?'

'Don't be ridiculous; it's all settled. Anyway, what difference is it to you if he's here or not?'

You grunt. There's no point in saying anything to her if she's made up her mind; she only gets cranky. You get the other deck-scrubber from the press and kneel down beside her and the two of you scrub backwards across the kitchen floor until you're at the sitting-room door. You both sing 'Babooshka' and push and pull the scrubbers across the floor in time to it, screeching out the waily bits. You're both roasting and knackered after and you flop onto the sofa in a big hot heap, breathing real loud.

'Thanks for helping with the floor,' she says.

'Why doesn't Anne's ma like Gwen's ma?'

Your ma doesn't answer for a while.

'Go on miss nosy posy, you don't miss a trick,' she says and hops up.

'It's just that Anne keeps going on about it.'

'Last one up the stairs is a rotten egg,' your ma shouts, and before you know what's happening she legs it out the door. When you get out into the hall, she's standing at the top of the stairs. Her face is kind of sad-looking. 'Kit and myself have decided to give it another go,' she says. You say 'Oh' and then she goes into Liam's room and you hear her telling the boys that Rory will be coming to stay. Liam's delighted.

11

Feet

Rory has smelly feet. Your ma can't cope; the stink is all over the house. You'd need a gas mask. It's not a hot smell, like the smell from something dead, like a fox. And it's not a fat smell either, like cheese. It's sharp and it gets inside your nose – and even your mouth – like a cold wind. Your ma tells him to leave his runners at the back door to air them. He leaves them on the windowsill upstairs instead – on the outside – mortifying you all in front of the world. She asks Kit to have a quiet word with him.

There's still no reply from Gwen and you're starting to wonder if your letter got lost on the way over to Wales. Maybe a sack of post fell off the ferry, into the oily water at the docks, before the boat even left Dublin. Or maybe the Welsh postman got tired carrying around so many letters and parcels and threw one bag away, and your letter just so happened to be in that bag. Or maybe you wrote the address wrong on the envelope.

'She still hasn't written back,' you say to your ma, who is pushing all the windows up to get Rory's stink out of the house. You follow her around.

'Who's "*she*" – the cat's mother?' She always says that if you don't mention the person's name, but you're not in the mood for her comments.

'Gwen! Gwen hasn't written back.'

'Oh,' she says and you can tell that she couldn't care less. She's all happy now that Kit's coming around again with his fecking sausages and puddings and hairy bloody bacon. 'Where's Rory gone with the boys?'

'How the hell should I know?' you roar.

She's full of remorse then and asks how would you like to go for a spin in Kit's Merc later on? You say that you would prefer to stay at home, thank you very much, but you don't really mean that. You're dying for another go in the car. She says 'Suit yourself,' not even giving you a chance to change your mind, and then she sprays air-freshener over your head which makes you sneeze.

Rory sucks up to Kit like mad. He keeps going on about how much the baby seems to like him, how they're great pals.

'They're cracked about each other altogether,' your ma says, but you think that's going a bit far.

Kit throws the baby up in the air and catches him. It makes the baby do a wobbly laugh. You don't like the way he tosses him up because it looks dangerous. Your ma doesn't like it either, you can tell, but all she says is 'Take it easy, Kit,' and he laughs. The baby laughs too; he chuckles away to himself and puts his fat arms around Kit's neck and gives him a love.

'The first name he says will be Kit,' Rory says.

'He already said his first name and it was Mama,' you say, setting him straight.

'But that's not really her name, is it?' says Kit. 'You and Liam always call her ma and everyone else calls her Joan.' He pulls on his moustache and looks at the baby. 'No, I'm inclined to agree with Rory; I'd say the first name he'll say *properly* will be Kit.'

You hate the way he wants to make everything all about himself. And Rory's worse for egging him on. He never knows when to shut his gob. When someone talks too much around Noel, he always says 'Shut your face and give your arse a chance.' You'd love to say that to Kit and to Rory, but you know that your ma would probably clobber you, so you don't bother to waste your breath.

After coming back from their drive in the car, the baby falls asleep in Kit's arms while he sits watching telly with your ma. You don't ask them where they went, not wanting to give Kit the satisfaction. You watch him kissing the baby's sweaty little forehead and patting his knobbly hair while he holds him. He nearly looks nice when he does that, like he really cares about the baby and your ma and all of you. But maybe not Rory, because he's fifteen and anyway, Kit barely knows him. You decide to go on up to bed because there is nothing on, only the news, which is full of boring stuff about hurling and Maggie Thatcher.

When you wake up in the morning there are nuggets of hard stuff stuck in the corners of your eyes. They feel like grains of sugar. Before you open your eyes, you pick them out and that helps you to wake up. It feels satisfying. When you are fully awake, you get an awful fright because Rory's sitting on the end of your bed, watching you. You pull your covers up to your neck and sit up a bit.

'What do you want?' you ask.

'Nothing. I'm having a look around.'

'Well, you can get out now.'

'I'll get out when I'm good and ready.' He pulls at your eiderdown. You hold onto it tight and you can feel your face getting really hot. 'Sap,' he hisses into your face, 'you're taking a reddener. Are you afraid I'll see your nightdress, little girl?'

You take a swipe at him but he lunges back and you miss. Because you've let go of the covers, he manages to pull them off you. He starts laughing his head off. The door opens and it's your ma. She stands in the doorway with her hands on her hips.

'Breakfast, Rory,' she says, her voice strangly.

'I was just going, Auntie Joan.'

He throws your covers back on top of you in a messy heap. Your ma looks at you and frowns, but she doesn't say anything and she goes off downstairs. You feel like you're being blamed for something; really it's Rory who should be in trouble for sneaking around the place and messing up your room.

When you go down for breakfast, he's shovelling cereal into himself like a pig. When your ma's not looking, he sticks his tongue out at you and it's covered in Weetabix. It looks disgusting, as if he's eating mud. Then Liam starts doing the same thing, but your ma catches him and slaps him on the hand. Liam starts crying and Rory's laughing and your ma shouts at the two of them to shut up, which they do. Rory gets a shock because your ma normally treats him very kindly and he's not used to her like that. You're glad at least that Kit isn't sitting there, smoking his stinky cigarettes, to add to the smell of Rory's feet and the bad-mood feeling.

Your ma lets you bring Liam on the bus into town to meet your da all by yourself. You're in charge of him. Liam says he doesn't want to go, but your ma makes him because she's going off in the car with Kit again. Cora says that they're like love's young dream, but she doesn't sound as if she's happy for them when she says it. The bus you get is one of the orange ones with blue seats. It's different to the old buses – tidy, with no graffiti on the walls and no chewing-gum stuck in black splodges all over everything. And the windows are sparkly clean. Liam's delighted to be on one of the new buses – it's his first time. He likes the way the doors open and close when the driver presses a button. He says he'd love a go of that button.

Your da hasn't got Clare with him, thank God, so the three of you can have some peace and quiet. Your da lets you pick a comic each in Eason's and you get one that includes a free necklace which your da clips around your neck. The beads are lovely: red and brown and blue and yellow. Your da says it looks really pretty on you. He says you're getting all grown up.

'So, how's Joan? And the baby?'

'They're grand,' you say.

'They're gone off for a jaunt with Kit,' Liam says, 'in his car.

It's a Mercedes and it's green.'

'Kit? Who's Kit?'

You stare at Liam, but he gawps at you like a moron. You weren't supposed to say anything about Kit. Or at least you weren't going to.

'Kit's Mammy's boyfriend,' Liam says, and you could kill him.

'Oh,' your da says, turning to look at you, but you smile at him and ask where he's taking you today. 'It's not Kit Nugent, is it? Not Noel's brother, not *that* Kit?' your da says. His face looks so serious all of a sudden.

'That's right,' Liam pipes up, 'Mammy's in love with Noel's brother and they're going to have a baby.'

'No, they're not,' you say to Liam. 'No, they're not,' you say to your da, but he doesn't seem a bit happy now, so you give Liam a dig. 'It's not true, Da. She's never having any more kids; she said it.'

'Kit Nugent. Of all the people in the world she goes and picks him.' Your da shakes his head.

'Thanks a lot,' you bark at Liam. 'Now he's going to be in a crap mood.'

'Now, now. I'm surprised, that's all. It won't stop us from enjoying ourselves.' He grabs the two of you by the hand, but his hold is too firm, so you drag your hand away before he breaks your fingers.

You don't enjoy yourself. Your da doesn't listen to anything you say. You tell him that the postman lost your letter to Gwen and he goes, 'Oh, really? That's nice'.

'It's not nice, it's a bloody scandal,' you say, and all he says is 'Hmm', not even commenting about the way you used the word bloody. He doesn't look around him, just keeps walking with his eyes looking in front. He brings you up to the Garden of Remembrance to look at the sad faces of the Children of Lir, who were turned into swans by their wicked stepmother. It's not much of a garden, but there are long pools of water that you can trail your hands through. They're not big enough to swim in though. Your da sits staring up at the Children of Lir while you and Liam play chasing between the water pools. Liam is nearly always on, because you are a fast runner and he isn't. But sometimes you feel sorry for him and go like a tortoise, so that he's able to catch you.

After that you have chips in a café on O'Connell Street. It's fancier than the one you usually go to, but your da is so quiet that it's hard to enjoy the food properly. Even the jelly and ice cream isn't easy to swallow with him looking all down and strange. Your da's normally quite jolly.

'Tell your ma to be in Cora's at six o'clock. I'll ring her for a chat,' he says, and gives you the envelope for her and a few bob for yourselves.

He puts you onto the bus at the quays. He tells you to make sure and sit downstairs, away from the smokers. You and Liam wave out the window at him, but he has already turned away and is disappearing into the crowds of people. Once he's gone, the two of you go up the stairs to sit on the top deck. You watch some seagulls swooping over the Liffey, diving down to the dark water to search for fish, and you wonder if grown-ups can ever be happy.

Rory has music blaring in the sitting room when you get back home. He doesn't hear you come in and he looks like a right eejit dancing around the place screeching 'Stories for Boys'. He obviously fancies himself as your man who sings that song, but he looks like a dope, not a bit cool or anything. He's doing all this stupid stuff, waving his arms over his head and jumping sideways and waggling his bum. You and Liam go into fits at the state of him. When he turns around and sees you, he says, 'What are you looking at?'

'A monkey, what's the charge?' you say, which is what your ma always says.

'I'll kill you,' he screams, and he chases you and Liam around the house. When he catches you he tiddles you under the arms until you nearly wet your knickers. Your face gets sore from laughing. Liam loves that kind of messing, but you are getting too big for it really.

When your ma and the baby get back, you tell her that your da's ringing Cora's at six o'clock.

'Oh. I wonder why?' she says, peeling off the baby's jacket. 'He only saw you today. Well, you'd better get on down to Cora's so and wait for him to ring.'

'No, Ma, it's you he wants to talk to.'

'Me? Did he give you the envelope?'

'It's in the press.'

'Well, I'd better go down to Cora's then,' she says and she leaves the baby with you.

Your auntie Bridget arrives while your ma's out.

'How's my sweetheart?' she says to Rory and tries to give him a kiss, but he pulls away from her. She gives Liam a kiss on the cheek which leaves the shape of her mouth in lipstick. She gives one to you too and it's cold. She asks Rory how he's getting on.

'Grand, but I'll get a lift home with you.'

'Your father needs a little more time to calm down,' Auntie Bridget says. It makes you wonder why your Uncle Jack is so mad with Rory that he has to stay at your house. 'Is Joan feeding you?'

'Ma!' Rory says.

'Well, well, look at you, quite the little lady,' your auntie Bridget says to you.

You're glad that you're still wearing the pink dress that you had on to go and meet your da. Your auntie is very particular about her appearance and she likes everyone else to be too. Normally you look a bit skacky, with old trousers on and your hair all over the place, but you look well today, even if you do say so yourself.

'Rory has stinky feet,' Liam says.

'Oh, I know all about it,' your auntie says and starts laughing. 'We'll never be able to do anything about Rory and his smelly runners!'

Rory grunts and gives Liam daggers; he'll be in for it when your auntie leaves. Your ma comes back.

'Don't mind me, Joan. I'm just on a little visit to my son and heir.'

'He's no bother,' your ma says.

'Joan,' Bridget says, 'will you not let me at those eyebrows? I'm dying to pluck them.'

Your ma runs her fingers over her eyebrows. 'So I can look like you, Bridget, is it?' she says, real smart. Your auntie Bridget has to draw in her eyebrows with a pencil because she pulled all the hairs out. Now there are two horrible creases, with two thin dark lines drawn over them.

'Well, you could at least let me tidy them up.'

'I've more on my mind than eyebrows,' your ma sighs, hooshing the baby onto her hip. Then Auntie Bridget makes a big show of giving your ma money.

'To keep Rory in the style he's accustomed to,' she says.

Rory groans and tells her to shut up and him and your auntie Bridget get into an awful row. Your ma brings you and Liam and the baby into the kitchen to leave them at it.

'What did you say to your da?' she says to you, closing the kitchen door and waggling her finger. You hate when she does that. You stare at her and let your eyes go dazed and swimmy so that you can't see her properly; she looks all blurry. When you don't answer, she says 'Well, anyway,' and goes to fill the kettle to make a cup of tea.

12

Doll Face

The way you hear the river, as it flows past your house all day and all night, is somewhere in the back of your head. Not at the front like a real sound. Sometimes you have to listen hard to hear it at all, you're so used to its noise. The river is like a secret. You own it, and you know all about the dead animals it carries, and the ducks and swans and sticks and scurf that float on it. You love looking out at the water and you think that you live in the best house in the world. Not that you've been in much of the world, but it's definitely the best house around where you live. It's the most special one because it's built right on the river; nearly in it.

Your ma hasn't been to many other places in the world either, but she collects foreign dolls. At least she used to when your da worked on the Continent. Every time he came back, he'd bring her a new doll, wearing the clothes of its own country, which is called a costume. She has them all on a shelf in her room. They get dusty, so you and your ma brushed them down once and wrapped each one in cling film to keep them clean. They're mostly girl dolls, but she has one boy doll who is part of a set of twins from Holland. They have blond hair and painted wooden clogs on their feet. They're the image of one another; identical. Your favourite of all the dolls is the one from Brittany in France. She has a high black hat – like something Fred Astaire would wear in a dancing film – and a white lacy ruffle around her neck. Her face is pretty: she has a tiny nose and bunched up lips which are pinky-red. You wish that your lips looked like that: pursed in a pout and the colour of raspberries. Yours are a bit flat and thin and ordinary.

Rory says you're ugly; he says he's never seen anyone as poxy-looking as you. Your ma says not to mind him, that he's angry at the world and he's just taking it out on you. But now you can't stop looking in the mirror in the hall every time you pass it, and you spend ages examining yourself at the dressing table in your room. Rory says that your eyes bug out of your head like an insect. He says you have fly eyes. You've looked at them for a long time and you think he's wrong; your eyes look perfectly normal to you. He follows you around the house whispering 'Ug-bug' at you, so you go outside to get away from him.

Anne's gone on holidays to her granny's house in Wicklow; you've no one to play with or talk to. She never even told you she was going, and her da couldn't wait for you to get lost when you called to the house; it was obvious. He said 'Ah hello there, Gwen,' and you didn't even bother to set him straight. He kept looking behind him into the hallway instead of at you so you just thanked him and left. Not that there was anything to say thanks for, considering he couldn't even get your name right.

You're bored, but instead of going down to your normal place by the river, you decide to go for a walk over the fields. There isn't much to see, but the long grass and overgrown bushes are nice and summery. In the winter the grass is sparse and there's big churns of muck everywhere which your boots get stuck in. At the moment the elderberry bushes have clumps of tiny white flowers on them, but no dark berries yet. When the berries come, you love squashing them up; there's thousands of them on every branch and the stems that hold them are the colour of red wine.

You're glad there are no horses in the fields these days; they are very nosy and sometimes they gallop right over to have a look at you and that frightens the shite out of you. Horses are so tall. You prefer cows; they're really lovely. They look like the plastic cows in the baby's farmyard set, white with black splodges all over them. They stand there chewing on mouthfuls of grass, and you think if you pushed them, they'd probably topple over and land on their sides with their legs stuck out straight, like the toy ones. Cows are really friendly up close and their dark eyes watch you. Their smell is sweet and warm: a mixture of grass and milk and poo. It's hard to believe that cows end up as stew and steak. Thinking about it puts you off eating meat. And Kit's the one who murders them in the butcher's shop, which makes you feel even sicker.

Your ma and Kit are talking about going away for a few days, just the two of them. She announces this in the middle of dinner.

'I say go for it,' Rory says. 'And don't worry, Auntie Joan, I'll keep a good close eye on the children.' He stares over at you.

'I'm not a child and I don't need you keeping an eye on me,' you say, mashing your spuds right down with your fork and ploughing them up again like a field.

'Oh, you're all grown up, are you? A big girl now?' Rory says.

'Shut your face, you leper.'

'Now, now. I've already asked Cora and Noel to keep an eye, and Cora might even stay over.'

Yourself and Rory groan. You agree on one thing, anyway.

'We can mind ourselves,' you say. 'We don't need Cora here. Or Rory.'

'I'm not leaving you with no one in charge for a weekend and that's final.'

'Can we not come too?' Liam asks.

You wouldn't mind it. You've never stayed in a hotel and you could even put up with Kit for a few days if you had to.

'It's away from you all I'm trying to get!' Your ma laughs and you think it's well for some, fecking off on holidays while you're stuck here with nothing to do. That Kit has some nerve, dragging your ma away from her family the split second he's back in the door.

You and your ma and the boys go to collect Cora after her first day at work in Anne's ma's hairdressers. Rory is watching the prisoners who won't eat on the news, and he's enjoying it, so he stays at home. Boys love anything to do with bad stuff, like wars and starving people and fighting. And anyway, he probably wouldn't be caught dead going for a walk with you and your ma and the boys.

The windows of Krazy Kutz are all steamed up, but you can look through the door, which is open. Cora is in there, sweeping up the piles of hairs that are on the floor. Her face is bright red and Mrs Brabazon's lording it over her, especially when she notices you all waiting outside.

'Would you listen to that bitch,' your ma says, and even though normally you hate when she says things like that, you have to agree with her. You feel angry on Cora's behalf when Mrs B says 'You missed a bit' to her and then laughs, as if she's making a joke. It's not funny and you all know it. Mrs Brabazon waves out the door and says to your ma, 'Cora'll be with you in a tick. And do you know what, Joan? She's a great little worker!' and then she does a big exaggerated wink.

Cora comes out after a while. 'My feet are bloody well killing me,' she says.

'It's your woman who'd be killing me,' your ma says, pushing the baby's pram very fast, which is what she does when she's angry.

'Ah, Mags is alright,' Cora says, lighting up a fag, but she doesn't look like she believes herself.

'I'd love to get that sweeping brush and break it across her stupid blondie head,' your ma says.

'So would I,' says Liam, and that makes everyone laugh.

Cora brings you all back to her house and your ma spoils her by insisting that she sits down in front of the telly while she makes her a cup of tea and a ham and mustard sandwich. That's Cora's favourite sambo and she likes the butter and the mustard to be spread on very thick.

'I feel like Lady Muck, getting my tea served up to me.'

Even you agree that she deserves it after her hard day at the salon.

'Well, will you stick it, do you think?' asks your ma.

'I don't know. Noel doesn't want me going out to work at all, but I'll go off my rocker if I have to hang around here much longer. It's lonely all day.'

'I can think of better places to spend my time than with Mad Mags Brabazon.'

'Ah well,' Cora says, and you can tell that she doesn't want to discuss it any more. 'So, when exactly are yourself and the quare fella off on your holliers?'

'You'd hardly call a weekend in Wexford a holiday, would you?'

'I suppose.'

'Well, we thought Friday evening, if that suited you for keeping an eye on this lot. And Rory, of course.'

'That's grand. So any luck getting rid of the feet smell?'

'Jesus, don't talk to me. It's like living in a cesspit; I've never smelled anything like it.'

Your ma and Kit are going to be staying in a caravan in Kilmuckridge, not a hotel after all. Still, you've never stayed in a caravan and you would love to try it out. They have miniature cookers and a little toilet and all. One of the other butchers who works with Kit owns the caravan and he's giving it to him for a lend. It's near the sea. Your ma loves the sea. She says she must have been a fish in a former life because she always likes to be near water. They'll probably go swimming at the beach, the lucky suckers. You can't imagine Kit wearing togs; he would look horrible.

'Well, Cora, we'd better skedaddle. I'm expecting Winnie to call in.'

'Oh. Winnie,' Cora says and puckers up her mouth, but your ma just ignores her.

Winnie is your ma's friend as well, but not like the way Cora is.

She's not always at your house drinking beer or watching telly. She only comes sometimes and she drinks tea at the table and talks to your ma about her daughters and sons and her grandchildren. Winnie is the same age as your ma, but she looks much older; she wears her hair in a bun and she always wears gold dangly earrings. She told you that they are called 'creoles' after an island far away. She got married when she was fourteen. That's only four years older than you. You'd hate to get married; you'd have to make all the dinners and sleep in a bed with your husband. He'd be snoring and kicking and pulling all the blankets off you. It'd be disgusting.

Winnie is a tinker. Some people call them itinerants but Winnie and her family like being called tinkers because that's what they are. It means someone who makes pots and buckets out of tin and that's what her father does. Her and all her family live in tiny houses and caravans, all dotted around a mucky park at the side of a wide road. Winnie's house is lovely and she always has false flowers in vases in the windows. And she's very nice; she brings loads of sweets for you and Liam and the baby.

There's only one thing you don't like about Winnie and that is the tufts of hair under her arms. They are darker than the hair on her head, which is kind of blondey-red. She has a habit of waving her hands in the air when she's making a point, and your eyes are glued to her armpits and those hairy bits. Your ma doesn't have them; she shaves that hair off as well as the hair on her legs. Kit says your ma has lovely legs and he loves to see her in a skirt and not slacks. That's what he says; not 'trousers' like any normal person, but 'slacks'. You hate the look on his face when he says that about skirts. You're always watching him, because someone has to keep an eye on him, to see what he'll try next. You wouldn't be surprised if he wanted to come and live in your house.

Your ma gives Winnie her tea in a cup with a saucer. It's the best china and it used to belong to your granny. The cups are white with dark red roses and a gold line around the rim, and the handles are so small you can hardly fit your finger into them. They don't hold much tea either, but they're special and lovely. Winnie asks you how you're enjoying your school holidays and you say that they're going fine.

'You must be dying to get back to school all the same,' Winnie says.

'I'm not.'

Winnie laughs and her creoles wobble. You wouldn't mind a pair of them. You'd like to get your ears pierced, but your ma says not until you're twelve and you can look after them by yourself. She says she's fecked if she's having you going around with scabby ears like half the young ones in Dublin. Anne Brabazon's ear went septic and there was all pus coming out of it and it was so disgusting. She had to let the holes in her ears close up after that.

'I hear you're going around with an awful old blackguard,' Winnie says to your ma.

'Who said that?' your ma asks, a bit narky, reefing the tea cosy off the pot and not even looking over at Winnie.

'Pa knows him,' Winnie says. Pa is her brother, not her father like you would think.

'He's no worse than many. He's Cora's brother-in law.' She pours the tea.

'Has he got any money?'

'Winnie!' your ma says, pretending to be annoyed. Then she laughs and says he's not loaded, if that's what she means. 'He's a butcher.' Then she tells her that she's going away with Kit for a few days.

Winnie tuts and shakes her head. 'It'll end in tears, Missus,' she says. She calls your ma 'Missus' sometimes, even though she knows her name is Joan.

'Ah, would you stop,' your ma says, stirring her tea so hard that the spoon keeps clanging off the side of the cup. She's obviously fed up with everyone going on about Kit, when she thinks he's the bee's knees. You're glad that Winnie is against him, because that means that she's on your side. You ask may you leave the table and your ma says to go on. You slip out through the yard, past the ivy bushes with their rubbery leaves and on down to the river where everything shushes quietly.

13

A Holiday For Your Ma

You and Cora and the boys stand at the door to wave your ma off. She looks gorgeous in her denim skirt with her hair just after being washed. It's soaking down her back, making a dark patch on her red T-shirt. Normally she'd dry her hair with the hairdryer, but she's late getting ready, as usual, and Kit's outside, bipping the horn of the car. She has packed her bag and it feels really weird to see it in the hall before she goes. You don't ever remember her leaving you all before, except for the time she ended up in hospital, and you didn't even know she'd be going that time. Watching her getting ready makes your stomach feel empty.

Your ma cuddles the baby and kisses him three times, the way French people do. Even though she's delighted to be going on holidays, you can tell she's feeling a bit sad too. The baby gives her a love; he hugs her around her neck and puts his head down on her shoulder.

'Mind him for me now,' she says, handing him to you. Then she tells you to behave yourself for Cora and Noel, and she says that if Rory is doing your head in, you're to go down to Cora's house. She kisses her fingers and puts the kiss on your nose. She gives Liam a big hug and he clings to her leg for a minute. She promises to bring him back something nice, like a stick of rock.

You had a stick of rock before which was green, white and orange on the outside and just white in the middle; the word 'Éire' went all the way down through it. You sucked the rock into a glassy point like a needle, and it was so sharp you could've stabbed somebody with it. Éire means Ireland and it's what they put on the back of the coins and on anything Irish. As far as you can remember, it was your granny who gave you that rock; it lasted for days because you rolled it back into the plastic wrapper each time you'd finished sucking it. It was deadly.

'Be good, all of you,' your ma says and Cora says you'll be grand. 'Good girl,' your ma says to you, and chucks you under the chin, before sitting into the car.

'Goodbye, Ma,' you call, and wave to her in the front seat of the Merc. Kit leans down across her, puts his hand on her leg, and gives you a slow wave out through the window. He has a smirk on his face that makes you feel like smacking him. He thinks he's 'it' with his horrible little moustache and his big car that isn't even properly his.

'Look at him,' Cora says through her teeth. 'You'd think butter wouldn't melt in his mouth, the big shite.' She waves. 'Bye now, Joan. Have a ball.'

Your ma looks happy, she's smiling in a way that she doesn't do very much. The smile gets into her eyes. She has lovely eyes; they're not blue and they're not grey, they're somewhere in between. They look like glass. You watch the car go up the road; it gets smaller as it goes, until it's just a pea-green blob, and then it disappears over the bridge. Cora puts her arm around your shoulder. She sighs.

'Noel has barely got a look in since they bought that car and, after all, he half owns it. I'm fed up going around in the fecking truck like an extra sack of coal, thank you very much, getting black muck all over my good clothes.' Cora grunts.

You all troop through the yard into the kitchen, which seems extra empty now that your ma's gone. You don't know what to be doing with yourselves. It's too early for dinner and there's nothing good on the telly. Rory is gone to practise with Neighbourhood Disturbance, his band, so he won't be back for ages. Cora says she's glad because the smell of his feet suffocates her; she doesn't know how you all put up with it. She folds her crooked arms across her chest, which is wide and big. Cora is what some people would call roly-poly, or in other words fat.

'Can we have some lemonade at your house?' Liam asks.

'Of course you can, that's a great idea.'

She straps the baby into his pram and she hooshes you out the door. You're glad Cora is with you because otherwise you think you might cry because you miss your ma so much already. That makes you feel a bit silly, so it's nice to go to Cora and Noel's house to take your mind off being homesick for your ma.

Cora sets you up at her kitchen table and gives you glasses of lemonade and some bickies. She even gives the baby a drop of lemonade and he thinks it's great, but then he drinks it so fast he gets a shock at the fizziness in his nose and he starts gasping. Liam jumps up and pats his little back so that he'll burp.

'Jesus, Mercy and Joseph,' Cora says when she hears the baby spluttering, but you explain to her that he's only just started drinking real milk instead of milk from your ma, so lemonade is mad to him. But anyway he definitely seems to like it, because next thing he's holding up his glass to Cora and saying 'This, this', which means he wants more. So she gives him another sup, just for the taste, holding the glass while he sips.

You ask Cora if she thinks that your eyes look wonky, like the ones on a spider or a fly.

'Get away out of that. What in God's name gives you that idea?' she asks.

'I don't know, they look funny sometimes, kind of weird,' you say, and you cross them on purpose when you look at her.

'Will you stop that! The wind will change and your eyes will be stuck that way for the rest of your days.'

You keep your eyes crossed by staring at where the end of your nose should be and opening them real wide, but after a while it's too much effort, so you stop. Then your eyes are achy. Cora says that your eyes are beautiful, exactly the same as your ma's, and you're delighted with yourself, but in a low way because now you miss your ma again.

'I want Mammy,' Liam says, and starts blubbering.

'There, there, stop that now or you'll have us all in bits,' Cora says, and she drags Liam onto her lap. She holds him close to her chest and you can see Liam staring at her knotty fingers. Cora has big soft legs and her lap is very comfy. You remember that from before, from when you were small.

'I'll tell you what,' Cora says. 'Why don't we all go on a picnic tomorrow down by the river? I'll make up a basket of goodies and we'll bring a blanket to sit on and it'll be lovely.'

You and Liam think that's a great idea. You tell Cora it's such a waste that she doesn't have any kids, because she would be a brilliant ma. She goes all pink and says 'Would you ever stop,' and she's laughing and all. She lights up a fag and lets the baby blow out the match and he's thrilled with himself. He keeps making blowing noises and spits dribble from his mouth all down his front.

You decide to make a list of stuff for the picnic. You and Liam sing 'One man went to mow, went to mow a meadow', and the baby claps his hands and Cora says 'That's a marvellous song,' while she gets some paper from the drawer to make the list on. All she has is an old copybook where Noel tots up the coal money and it's black with his fingerprints. She sees you looking at it.

'It'll do,' she says. 'Beggars can't be choosers.'

You make the list because you're the best writer – you got eighty-five per cent for handwriting in school – and the things you put on it are ham sandwiches, cheese sandwiches, lemonade, crisps, apples (Cora's idea), chocolate, biscuits, beer for Noel (Liam's idea), a flask of tea (Cora says she'll have to root out the flask) and rusks for the baby (your idea). You all agree that that sounds like a fantastic picnic and now you can't wait for the next day. Cora says to bring your swimming togs and a couple of towels, just in case.

Liam says, 'Just in case what?'

'In case it's a nice day, silly,' you say, and Cora nods.

Then she walks you all home to your own house, even though it's still bright and you would be fine by yourselves. Still, it's good of her to care so much about your safety. The baby falls asleep in the pram and he doesn't even wake up when you and Liam sing the 'Went to mow a meadow' song loudly. Cora gets to know the words and she joins in on the last bit of each line, which kind of puts you off, but you don't spoil things by asking her not to sing. You fall in the door, laughing.

Rory has a girl in your sitting room.

'Does your auntie Joan know you're entertaining guests while she's away?' Cora says, real cool, to Rory.

'She said I could bring my friends over if I wanted to,' Rory says, stretching his legs out along the sofa and putting his arm around the girl's shoulder. The girl's really gorgeous-looking, with blonde hair like a doll's, but you think she must be off her trolley to be sitting so close to Rory. 'This is Veronica.'

Cora says 'Hmmph' and Veronica giggles.

'Veronica, meet Cora Nugent, the neighbour,' Rory says. 'And these are the saps.'

'Now Rory, you be nice to your cousins,' Cora says.

'He doesn't bother us, Cora,' you say, and your woman Veronica giggles again and it's obvious to you that she's a dope. You stand there, gawking at them, feeling like a visitor in your own house, and you wish you could boss Rory around. How dare he bring a young one into your ma's house without even asking her. The cheek of him.

'We're going on a picnic tomorrow, Rory,' Liam says. 'Will you come?'

'Of course I'll come, sport,' Rory says and you could murder Liam and his big fat mouth.

'I'd better be going; Noel will be looking for his tea.' Cora smiles at you, then warns Rory to behave himself. You walk her out into the hall and she says that Rory is a brat and to come and get her and Noel if there's any funny business.

'How do you mean?'

'You know, upstairs business,' Cora says, but you're not sure exactly what she's on about.

You're raging that Rory might be coming with you on the picnic, but you don't say that to Cora. You say cheerio and go back inside to lift the baby up to bed. Veronica says she's going to head off, and Rory says he'll walk her to the bus stop. You bring the baby upstairs and dress him for bed and he hardly wakes up. His hair is damp from where he was lying back in the pram and you smooth it down with your fingers. You hop into your ma's bed with him. Liam gets in too and even though you think you'll never sleep because your ma's not there, you go out like a light.

The morning fills your ma's room and you can see that it's going to be a lovely day, which means you'll get to go for a dip in the river. Not too far in though, because there could be anything hiding in the river-weed. Like eels. And in some places there's a load of broken bottles and they could cut your feet to ribbons and that'd be the end of your big day out. You are so excited about the picnic that you don't mind getting the boys ready. The baby knows something fun is happening and he's so happy wiggling about the place and laughing. You unzip him from his fuzzy blue pyjama-suit that makes him look like a teddy bear. Your ma insists that he wears it, even though it's the summertime, because he always kicks the covers off himself at night. She thinks he might catch a chill.

The baby is long and thin, even though his arms and legs are quite puddingy. You love the buttery smell of him and the way everyone says he's gorgeous with his brown skin and his black, black eyes. He has fallen in love with a toy dog of Liam's and he says 'Woof-woof' every time he sees a real dog now. He's such a smart baby. You spoon his brekky into him, so that you'll all be ready quicker. You hope that Rory will stay in bed, but next thing he's standing there in his manky brown pyjamas, yawning his head off.

'Going without me, Little Miss Prim?' he says and you just give him a filthy look and carry on feeding the baby. 'Well, Liamo, will we go fishing?'

Liam is delighted; he thinks Rory is God. Rory puts the kettle on and says that with any luck the brown bear in the woods hasn't caught all the fish and eaten them up for his own breakfast. You tut out loud and throw your eyes up to heaven, because there's no such thing as bears in Ireland. Not since millions of years ago. You butter some toast for Liam and tell him to hurry up.

'Relax,' Rory says; 'the river isn't going anywhere.'

'Feck off out of my face and mind your own business,' you say.

He puts his nose right up to yours and laughs. You can smell his bed-breath and it makes you want to puke.

14

Picnic

The spot Cora chooses is beside the mud path, a bit back from the bank that leads down to the water's edge. Noel makes a song and dance of laying out the groundsheet first and then putting the blanket on top of it. He keeps saying he knew that the groundsheet would come in handy one day, and Cora says would he for God's sake ever stop going on about it. The blanket is a red tartan one, lovely and soft, but there's hardly room for everyone's bum on it because Rory stretches himself out fully on one side. He's such a pain; you're mortified with the way he goes on.

The sun is silver and hot; it makes the river dazzle. You and Cora cover the picnic basket with your cardigans to keep the heat off it until it's time to eat.

'This is the life,' says Noel and he lies back on the other side of the blanket and closes his eyes. He's wearing shorts that used to be jeans, and an old vest. He looks like a disaster, but Cora doesn't seem to mind. She's used to him; he always looks terrible because he's a coalman. He just looks awful in a different way in shorts.

'Indeed and it is the life,' says Cora. 'Your mammy doesn't know what she's missing.'

You smile instead of answering. You don't want Liam thinking too much about your ma, so you help him to put on his togs, holding the towel around him to make sure no one can see. He keeps jumping and skitting, saying everyone's looking at him. You have to keep pulling him back towards you in case he falls over. When Liam is ready, he wraps himself in his towel and sits up on the blanket beside Rory.

'I believe you have a new mot,' Noel says. Rory grunts. 'I hear she's smashing looking altogether.'

'She's not bad,' Rory says, trying to sound cool. You think he sounds like a thick.

'Well, she must be off her bin to be hanging around with you,' you say.

'Yeah, off her bin,' Liam says and Cora laughs. Rory leans over and swipes at Liam, but misses, swiping at the air instead.

'Where is she today,' Noel asks, 'this beauty of yours?'

'I dunno. She's working, I suppose.'

'Oh, that's the way to have them alright,' Noel says. 'Show them who's boss.'

'Stop putting ideas in Rory's head,' Cora says.

You strip the baby and put a pair of shorts on him and then you carry him down to the river. You paddle in and hold him over it, letting his toes dangle into the water. It's cold, so you only let him stay in for a minute. He kind of loves it and hates it at the same time. He squeals when his feet touch the water, but when you lift him onto your hip again, he points at the river and says 'This, this'. Then he tries to put his toes in by himself. Cora keeps calling you back; she doesn't like the baby being near the river. After a few more little dips, you lift him back onto the bank and climb up yourself. Cora wraps the baby in a towel and holds him on her lap. She plays peek-a-boo with him and he thinks it's great gas. Cora loves the baby.

You go back down to the water with Liam. He has his net-on-a-stick with him and he's hoping to catch something. You show him the little clumps of minnows that are crowding in the shallows. But when he tries to catch them, they swim away real fast before he has a chance to put the net under them. Then he churns up the river muck and you can't see them at all. Noel tells him to have his jam jar ready to put them into, so he goes to get it.

You stay in the water and let the mud squidge through your

toes. It feels lovely: all squishy and cool, like wet cake-mix. You look across the river to the low road on the other side and think about the day you all went for the jaunt to The Strawberry Hall in the green Mercedes. You wonder if your ma is having a nice time on her holidays.

Cora calls 'Why don't you put your togs on?'

You don't want Rory gawping at you. 'I'm fine for the moment; I don't feel like swimming yet,' you call back.

Rory's still sprawled all over Cora's blanket, listening to his transistor. He has his eyes closed and is mouthing the words to the song that's playing. He thinks he's great. Cora's left with the bare edge of her own blanket to sit on and she has the baby to mind and all. Noel starts rummaging under the cardigans that are covering the picnic basket.

'What are you at?' Cora says, pushing Noel's hand off the basket and covering it up again.

'Would you go away out of that,' Noel says, pulling the basket over to himself and getting out two bottles of beer and a pack of playing cards.

'Well, it's a bit early for that carry on,' Cora says. Noel hands Rory a bottle of beer and Cora shakes her head. She lights up a fag. 'Don't be feeding drink into him,' she says.

'Relax,' Noel says and that gets Cora's goat. She puffs on her fag very fast.

'Will you come for a little walk with me?' she says to you, 'I need to stretch my pins.' She tells Noel to keep an eye on Liam and the baby.

You tell Liam to watch out for the crabs and lobsters that live in the river, and to mind that they don't bite his toes. He looks so worried that you have to tell him you're only messing. You put the baby's nappy and T-shirt back on and give him a quick cuddle and kiss before you go. He sits on the blanket between Liam and Rory, watching Noel dealing out the cards, and he waves at you when you say bye-bye. He looks happy with himself because he loves hanging around with men. Not that you'd call Rory a man.

Cora walks slowly and she huffs and puffs because she's not great on her legs. She sucks on the end of her fag.

'I'm like the wreck of the Hesperus,' she wheezes. Whatever that is, you think. 'As long as I don't end up like poor daddy, Lord rest him. He was only fifty when he lost his walk.'

She's wearing a big floppy straw hat and it makes her look like a banana boat; you wish she'd take it off. By the time you walk a little way down the field with Cora, you're fed up. She crawls along and she never stops talking. You're dying for the picnic; the idea of it is burning a hole in your head. Thinking about the sandwiches and all the other food makes your mouth fill with spits, which is a sure sign that you're weak with the hunger. Cora's going on about her new job and Mrs Brabazon and how it's roasting all the time in Krazy Kutz, especially because of the heatwave. She says that Mags Brabazon is as tight as a hen's arse because she won't plug in the two air-fans, which would cool the place down a bit.

'And I wouldn't mind only she's loaded. It's not as if she can't afford the electricity bill. God, she makes me sick.' Cora's getting really wound up. 'But anyway, it's a little job for me and it passes the time.' First Cora hates Mrs B and her job, then she loves everything about it; she should make up her mind.

'I'd like being a hairdresser,' you say.

'I suppose your mammy deserves a treat,' Cora says then. One second she's on about one thing and then she's straight on to the next.

'I suppose,' you say, wondering if she means that being away with Kit is meant to be a big treat. You'd rather swallow rusty nails.

You're thinking about how nice it would be to be lounging on the blanket like Rory, sipping a cool drink and playing snap, instead of rambling with Cora, who is a snail. There are big flat cow poos all over the place and you have to pick your way around them. Some of the cowpats are hidden in the thistles; you walk on ahead and point them out to Cora so that she won't walk in them. When you go too near them, all the fat brown flies fly off and the look of them makes you sick. Some of the poos have grey horseflies stuck to them and they'd sting you as soon as look at you. You wonder how there are so many poos – such fresh ones – when there aren't any cows to be seen. You finally get to the end of the field, where the footbridge goes over the river, and you both turn around to go back. Cora sighs and waddles, and then she starts doing soft grunts through her nose. She's getting totally exhausted. That's what happens to fat people – they are heavy, even to themselves.

'I'm dying for my bit of lunch now,' she says.

'Me too.'

'Maybe they'll have it laid out?' Cora says and the two of you look at each other and laugh, knowing there's no way any of them would dream of having the picnic ready. It'll be up to Cora and you, and you like it better that way.

You can see Rory and Noel like two dots in the distance. You can't make out where Liam and the baby are. There's a flapping in the reeds near to you, so you run over to the bank and see two moorhens fighting. You love their bright red beaks and black feathers; they're such posh-looking birds.

'What's Noel at?' Cora says, when you get closer to the others. She stops to shade her eyes from the sun and squints to get a better view. 'What's that on the grass?'

You look up to where they are. They've all moved. They're right on the side of the riverbank now. You can see Liam. He's standing near to where Noel and Rory are kneeling on the grass, looking down. Liam is staring at the ground too, and he's not moving.

'Liam must've caught a fish,' you say. 'Or a lobster.'

Cora doesn't laugh or say anything. Next thing you see Rory jump up from the grass; he starts shouting. He's pulling his own hair and bending over nearly double. He's screeching and the sound carries down to you in a long, loud loop, like an echo. Cora starts to run.

'Oh Jesus, oh no!' she says and she's running along, not going very fast, and her arse wobbles under her dress. She's calling out, but it's only like a whisper. 'Oh Jesus, please no,' she says over and over. Her sun hat falls off and she doesn't even stop to pick it up. You start to run too and you get ahead of her. When you come near to them, Rory lunges at you and pushes you away.

'Get back,' he shouts, and he grabs your arms and holds them to your sides. All his clothes are wringing wet and water-drops drip from his hair on to your face. You wriggle out of his grip and push away his hands.

'Get off me, Rory,' you say, shoving him in the stomach, and then you stare at him. He's acting like such a weirdo. He stands there, looking back down the field to where you've just come from. When you dash past him, he doesn't even turn or try to stop you.

The baby's lying on the grass. His head's flopped to one side and his eyes are half-open. He's as wet as a fish and there are streaks of mud on his legs. Liam's standing looking down at him and he's not saying or doing anything. Noel's kneeling on the grass beside the baby, covering his face with his hands, and he's whimpering. Cora comes up; she's wheezing like an old dog and sort of moaning and crying, all at the same time. She goes over to Noel and she starts thumping him around the head.

'You stupid bastard! You bastard!' she screams, and Noel doesn't even try to fight back. He lets Cora hit his head, and his whole body shakes and shakes.

Liam starts to cry. Your feet are stuck to the grass; all you can do is stand there and stare. Rory brushes past you and pulls the cardigans off the picnic basket. He lays them out on the blanket and then picks the baby up and gently wraps him in them. The baby doesn't move; he doesn't cry out or wriggle. Rory hands him to you. The baby feels light and heavy at the same time. You cup his head onto your elbow to stop it lolling and touch his eyelids to close them down. His skin feels cold under your fingers.

Rory runs on ahead of you towards the house. Cora and Noel walk slowly in front of you, holding Liam's hands. No one says anything and you hold the baby's body to yours, kissing his wet face all the time while you stumble through the fields to home.

BOOK TWO

1

Dog

When you live in a flat there's no garden or proper front door. You're miles up in the sky. You'd think it would be calm up there, but lots of noises hang around in the air. When you live in a flat you don't have a milkman. The milkman at home is called Leo. He wears a caramel-coloured coat and he sings and clinkety-clinks the milk bottles when he goes around. Leo's truck is huge, but he drives real slow. He lets you and Liam help him to deliver the milk and scut on the back of the truck. The birds love to break the lids of the bottles with their beaks and suck the cream off the top of the milk. You put stones on the lids to scare them away. Leo says you're a great help altogether. You might marry Leo when you grow up, if he's still alive.

Geraldine has a dog and he lives in the flat. His name is Sinbad and your da hates him. He calls him names like 'Sinister' and 'Sinful' and that drives Geraldine mad. Sinbad is chubby, he's tiny and his fur's grey and lumpy. He's well named because he's always doing bad sins like pooing on the stairs and in the lift. Your da's heart is broke with him. Sinbad's poos are pale, as if he eats nothing but white bread. Really he eats bowls of Winalot, which is a sort of breakfast cereal for dogs, and anything else that anyone gives him. He's a greedy little pig.

It's your job to bring Sinbad for a walk. At first you hated it, but now at least it gets you out of the flat and away from Geraldine, who's always moaning, and Clare, who's always hanging around your ankles. She's worse than any dog. Your da and Geraldine are not supposed to have a dog in their flat. There are no pets allowed, so you have to be extra careful when you're bringing Sinbad out during the day, in case there's anyone from the Corporation sniffing around.

Sinbad hates the stairs and he hangs around at the lift door waiting for it to open. But mostly it's broken, so he has no choice. All along the stairs and on the landings there's the stink of old wee. Sometimes you have to carry Sinbad down the stairs because he won't move his fat arse; you hate the feel of his hard, hairy body. He doesn't mind being picked up, but he smells rotten, so you only do it as a last resort. Other times, if he won't go down the first few steps, you give him a little kick, just to get him moving. Geraldine would go nuts if she saw you kicking her precious dog, but if she loves him so much, why doesn't she bring him out herself? But even though he's smelly and stuff, he's kind of a happy little dog and you love the way he goes nutty, wagging his tail and leaping about when anyone comes in to the flat. Sinbad's basket is out on the balcony, but your da says he's allowed inside when it rains.

The flat's baking hot. Your da says that the Corpo leaves the heating on day and night, winter and summer, and no one can do anything about it. There's no switch to turn it off or down. Geraldine's boiling all the time and she's cracking up. Her belly's all roundy because her new baby is in there, but it'll be coming out soon. About a trillion times a day she says 'I'm passing out with the heat.' But she never does.

Your throat feels dry all the time, especially at night. Yourself and Liam drink gallons of water and then you have to get up in the night to do a pee. But sometimes Liam wets the bed, because he's afraid of the corridor that leads to the loo. At home the bathroom's beside his room, so it's not so bad, there's some chance of him making it. But the corridor is long and spooky in the flat, and it's dark, because Geraldine can't sleep if the light is on. It drives

Geraldine nuts when Liam wets the bed because then she has to wash the sheets and hang them off the balcony to dry.

Liam's not really saying anything, not talking. It's like the time he got the mumps and his cheeks were all swollen up and he looked like a squirrel. You called him 'Mumpy' and your ma said 'That's not a very nice thing to say to your sick brother, now, is it?' Liam lay on the sofa for days and didn't open his gob. He just stopped talking altogether. He's like that in the flat.

Liam crawls into your bed most nights for a cuddle and that's the only time he makes a noise. He cries a lot at night. You pet his hair and tell him it'll be alright, but really you sometimes cry yourself. You love Liam and you are fed up with the way Geraldine's always screaming at him. And your da's no help. He only says 'Ah, leave him be,' to Geraldine. If you were him, you would tell her to shut her bleeding face. Your da says she's only in bad form because she's fed up waiting for the baby to come. He says she's uncomfortable in her skin at the moment.

Your ma was like a bag of clothes walking around, before she had to go back into the hospital for a rest. She couldn't eat a thing and Cora and Winnie were trying to help her swallow little bits, but she would vomit them back up. Winnie stayed at your house to keep an eye on your ma. Cora wanted to stay as well, but your ma wouldn't let her. Under your ma's eyes was all puffed up and black and she was going around staring into the air the whole time. She didn't want to go out and she didn't want to stay in. She sat in the kitchen drinking cups of tea, even if they were cold. And she kept her back to the window, with the blind drawn all the time, so that she couldn't see the river.

There's no river and no trees or grass where your da lives. There's only blocks of flats, a few shops and tons of roads. There's a smell like wet cement everywhere. The airport's very near and the rumbling sound of the aeroplanes going over at night makes you feel lonely. You wonder about all the people who go on planes to foreign countries; you think what lucky suckers they are. Liam's afraid that one of the planes will crash into the flat because it's so high up. But your da says that has never happened and it's never going to. Thank God for that, is all you can say.

Your da's off doing a nixer for someone in one of the other blocks, and Geraldine and Clare are having a nap. Liam's sitting watching telly.

'Do you want to come out for a walk with me and Sinbad?' you say. Liam shakes his head. 'Are you sure?' He shakes his head again. 'Fair enough.'

You get Sinbad's lead from the hook in the kitchen and call out to him. The lead stinks of soggy leather and dog. There's no sign of him jumping up, so you open the balcony door, which is really a window. Sinbad looks at you with big eyes, scratches behind his ear with his leg, and then pulls himself out of his basket and follows you to the hallway. You tell Liam not to answer the door to anyone and he stays on the sofa, staring at the cartoons; he doesn't even look over at you. You like the clicky noises that Sinbad's claws make on the floor outside the flat; it sounds like dancing. The lift's working for once, so he's in a happy-doggy mood, his stumpy tail wagging away.

Your da asked you to go to the shops and get milk before he left to do the bit of work for the neighbour. He gave you money from the tin that he keeps in the wardrobe. He likes giving you things to do because he knows there's no one to play with in the flats. The place is full of babies; there's no one your age. There are a few boys the same age as Liam, but Geraldine says they're dog-rough and she doesn't want Liam hanging around with them. All their hair's real short – they're skinners – and they have dirty faces.

There's only one facecloth between everyone in your da's flat.

It's raggy and it smells manky, like dead leaves. It makes you sick so you don't use it. You wash your face, and Liam's, with the corner of a towel. You tell him not to say anything to Geraldine, who might be quite happy to wash her face with a dirty cloth, but that doesn't mean that you are.

The shops are underneath the flats and the shutters are always pulled down, even when the shop's open. There's a hairdressers (not as nice as Krazy Kutz), a bakery and a sweet shop. They had to close down the chemist's because it kept getting robbed by baddies. The sweet shop sells papers and cigarettes and other stuff, as well as sweets, and the bakery smells gorgeous when you go past. You get the milk in the sweet shop and when you come out there's a gang of young ones outside. They have old faces. You have to stop to let Sinbad do a wee against a pole. He won't move until you let him go; he takes ages.

'What're you looking at?' one of the girls says, but you don't say anything. You pull Sinbad's lead and tell him to come on. 'The state of you,' the girl says. She's real common.

Your da told you not to talk to anyone at the shops except the shopkeeper. You yank at Sinbad's lead again, but he's too busy sniffing at other dogs' wee, which has dried into the pole and the ground.

'I love your dog, he's a beaut,' one of them says, real smart, and the rest of them start laughing. You can feel your neck getting scaldy. One of them comes over to you; she's really skinny and she's chewing some gum. She grabs the bottle of milk out of your hand and, before you can do anything, she drops it onto the ground and it smashes. You can't believe your eyes.

'Oh, whoops,' she says and puts her face up beside yours and snaps a bubble with her chewing-gum.

The path's covered in glass and a big puddle of milk. Sinbad starts licking at it. You're afraid the glass will cut his tongue, so you reef him by the lead and run off. You're doing gaspy crying and you only realise it when you can hardly breathe and there's tons of snots dripping from your nose. You're nearly choking Sinbad, who's not used to running at all. You stop at the bottom of your da's block of flats to catch your breath and look behind. They didn't follow you and you're glad, because you'd hate if they saw you crying. You're hiccupping now and you can't stop the tears that are rolling out of you like a fountain. Sinbad's looking at you like a moron and wagging his tail, and that only makes you cry more. You wish you could see your ma.

You hear someone calling 'Yoo-hoo' and you think it sounds like Cora, and then you get a shock because it *is* Cora and she's walking right up in front of you. You throw yourself at her and give her a hug and you get a noseful of her smell, which is fags and grease and roses, all in a mixture.

'My God, what's wrong with you, pet?' she says, when she sees you crying.

'Sinbad was peeing and then the milk broke; they broke the milk, and Sinbad nearly got cut,' you say, but you can hardly breathe with the gasping and the crying, and you even cry a bit harder so she'll feel sorrier for you. Cora wipes your face with her white hanky and she doesn't even mind that it gets covered in snots.

'Hang on now a sec,' Cora says and she shouts at Noel that she's going to go up to the flat with you. Noel's standing at the Merc having a fag and he waves over. You wave back and you think that he looks awful lonely. You ask if he's going to come up. 'He's staying with the car,' Cora says. 'You'd never know what class of gurrier they have around here.'

Cora takes your hand, and hers feels so soft, like something from home, and you can't help putting your lips to the back of it, in a half-kiss. You're dragging Sinbad behind you and he's still trying to pee; he must have the most enormous bladder in the universe to be able to go so much. You're glad the lift is working because Cora would pass out if she had to go up all those stairs. She says that she was up already, but there was no one home, and you're happy that Liam obeyed you, even though he could have let Cora in, no problem.

'Have you been to see my ma?' you say.

'I have, pet, but she's not feeling the best still and she doesn't want any visitors, for the moment.' You were hoping that Cora was going to bring you to see your ma, but you don't say that. 'She was asking for you and Liam,' Cora says gently and that makes you cry again. 'I have something for you here,' she says and starts rooting in her bag. She pulls out an envelope that's all crumpled and hands it to you. You see the stamp with the Queen's head through the tears in your eyes and you know immediately that it's from Gwen. You're dying to read it, but decide to save it up for when you're on your own.

When Liam sees Cora, he jumps off the sofa and wraps himself around her. Cora goes all wobbly because she's so happy to see him too. She gives Liam a kiss and lets him lie up in her lap on the sofa. Liam starts sucking his thumb like a baby. Like the baby.

'I was hoping to have a word with your father or Herself.' That's what she calls Geraldine, 'Herself'. 'It's a pity they're not in.'

'Geraldine *is* in, she's having a rest.'

Cora humphs. 'Well, I'll just wait until she decides to get up then. Myself and Noel are going to bring you for a spin in the car. We might go out as far as Dún Laoghaire and have a look at the boats.'

You're thrilled and so is Liam. It would be lovely to be out for a while in clean, fresh air, smelling the sea. Liam could certainly do with it. You decide to knock on Geraldine's bedroom door to tell her and it turns out she's been wide awake the whole time, lying in the bed and listening to the radio.

'Why didn't you tell me she was here?' Geraldine hisses at you, when you say that Cora's in the sitting room. She rolls off the bed and into her dressing gown. Geraldine doesn't bother to get dressed some days because none of her clothes will close over her bump. You say that Cora's only just arrived, but Geraldine pushes past you, mad impatient. You hear her saying hello to Cora, pretending she's in a great mood, but at least she says that you can go off in the car. 'It'll do them good, the poor little lambs,' Geraldine says.

2

Funeral

The baby's father came to the funeral. His name's Jonah and he's as black as a wet bog. He didn't talk much, but when he said hello to you his voice was very deep and trembly, like someone from a film. He shook your hand and his hand was huge. He spent the whole time following your ma around, but she was lost inside herself and she hardly even spoke to him. She had to introduce him to everybody, one at a time, and you could see them all looking. Your ma's hands were shaking and, even though it was a boiling hot day, she kept saying that she was freezing.

Your ma didn't want the baby left the whole night in the funeral parlour or the church, so she brought him home. She said she couldn't stand the thought of him in a dark place, all by himself, with no one to mind him. His coffin was white: a tiny little box. He was wearing his fluffy blue pyjama suit and he looked lovely, like as if he was asleep. He had his Big Bird toy in there with him and his own little blankie to cover him up. Your ma put the coffin on the table in the sitting room and everyone gathered around and said prayers. Liam stood beside the baby, guarding him. He rubbed a dirty patch with his fingers onto the satin lining beside the baby's head. The priest was nice – he had a kind face – and there was an old nun there too who was some relative, but you had never seen her before in your life.

Winnie and Cora made loads of sandwiches and brought them to your house. They had them all laid out on their own plates, with apple tarts and tea and lemonade. You only ate one sandwich –

you didn't feel a bit hungry – and it was even hard to swallow, because your neck was all tight. Liam didn't eat anything either and normally his tummy's a bottomless pit. You wandered from room to room looking at all the people in the house. Kit and Noel were in the kitchen smoking fags; your ma had banned it in the sitting room because the baby was there. They weren't talking to each other. Noel looked even worse than usual and you could see the hairy skin on his big belly because his shirt was too tight and it pulled open. He sat on a chair, his head hanging, smoking and letting out sighs. Kit stood by the window staring down at the river. He kept flicking his cigarette, but there was no spare ash to flick off. He looked at his watch a few times.

The sitting room was full of murmurs. People were whispering to each other and giving your ma hugs and saying 'The poor little thing,' and 'He's with the holy angels,' then they'd have a cry. You thought your ma's tears were all dried up, but then she'd start again, very quiet, and they would roll down her cheeks. Sometimes she'd stand beside Liam and the baby; other times she'd sit on the sofa, her eyes lost in the air. Jonah stood near her wherever she was. He didn't know anyone else.

Cora didn't go near your ma; she stayed standing up, watching. You and Winnie brought around the sandwiches to everyone. Some people ate loads. Like your Uncle Jack – Rory's father – who took handfuls of them at a time. Your auntie Bridget didn't eat anything; she said she was watching her figure and then she patted her stomach. Afterwards, in the kitchen, Winnie said that the two of them were disgusting people – Bridget and Jack – and that they made her sick. Rory was there, wearing a brown suit that made him look very grown up. You thought he'd be raging at what Winnie said, but he actually agreed with her. Winnie did a strangly laugh when she realised that Rory was their son. Then she went quiet.

When you offered the plates of food to people, they looked at you with sad eyes and you knew their hearts were breaking over the baby, and that they were full of pity for you and Liam and your ma. And maybe even Jonah. But you didn't want them feeling sorry for you. You wanted the baby back and the day not to be happening at all. But that was impossible.

When nearly everyone was gone, Winnie put Liam to bed and he went up, no problem. You thought he'd kick up a stink, but he was too tired to give out. Cora and Kit and Noel were the only people still there. Your ma and you sat on the sofa and they sat on chairs and you all stared at the walls, the carpet and each other. You could hear the clock going tick-tock, tick-tock, very loud.

'Joan,' said Noel, and then he stopped. 'Joan,' he said again, and then he started to cry; big fat tears fell down his nose and he was shaking.

'It's OK, Noel,' your ma whispered, not lifting her eyes to him. 'I'm not laying the blame at anyone's door.' Her mouth looked tired as she said the words.

That only made Noel worse and suddenly the whole lot of them were crying. Except Kit. He just lit up a fag. Your ma looked up at him and he left the room. You couldn't stand them all snuffling and crying with their big red faces, so you went over to say goodnight to the baby. When you kissed his cheek he felt stiff and cold, not like himself at all.

You couldn't sleep, so you stayed awake listening to the river rushing along. Your eyelids were stiff from crying and your body felt itchy all over. Your hair was prickling you – it was stingy and stuck to your head – and the whole bed felt crumby. After a while you got up and went to the window. For the first time ever you felt afraid of the water; it looked black and angry, and you thought you could see whirlpools turning on it. Liam came into your room and, without even noticing you standing at the window, he snuggled himself into your bed. There were no sounds in the house and all you could think about was the baby, lonely and small in his coffin downstairs. You climbed into the bed beside Liam and it was good to be safe under the blankets. You fell asleep. For a second – when you woke up in the dark – your mind felt clear; then you remembered what had happened, and thinking about the baby would make you cry all over again. That went on for the whole night.

In the morning your ma was lying on the sofa with her good coat thrown over her. She had moved the tiny coffin so that it lay beside her on the floor and her hand was resting on the baby's belly. Her face was as white as paper. You put out the Weetabix for everyone, but it ended up going dark and hard in the bowls, because none of you were in the mood for it. Your ma drank a cup of tea and then the men in the black cars came. They brought in the lid for the coffin. When your ma saw it, she shouted 'No! No!' and the man told you to bring her and Liam upstairs. You helped your ma get dressed and she was kind of wailing and catching her breath and you had to shove her arms into her jacket sleeves, because she just sat there, all floppy like a rag-doll. You put her hair in a ponytail because it was disastrous-looking – all bushy and sticking out. When you had Liam ready, you all went downstairs and your da was there and he put his arms around your ma and she started bawling.

You had your navy dress on. You were going to wear the white gloves you got for your Communion as well, but you didn't think your ma would like that. Anyway it was a bit hot for gloves. You wore them to your granny's funeral and you waved at everyone with them, moving your hand like a queen, but you were a bit old for that now. People might look at you funny. Liam wore his Communion suit, which is also navy. He was the youngest child in the school to make his Communion – he was only six and a bit – and you were all dead proud of him because he did a reading. The suit didn't look the same on him any more, probably because he was so quiet and everyone felt sad and blank.

Your da came in the big black car with you and your ma and Liam. And Jonah. Your ma was clinging on to your da, so he said he would come with her to the church. Geraldine stood near the house, rubbing her roundy belly and trying not to look put out. There were loads of people standing around the street – even neighbours you didn't really know – and it was nice of them to be there to see you off. The car was lovely on the inside – even nicer than the green Merc – and if you all hadn't been feeling upset, you probably would have really enjoyed being in it.

The church was full of candles, and their hot, drippy smell made you feel a bit woozy. The organist was playing tunes quietly in the background. You were up the front with your ma and da and Liam and Jonah and all your other relatives. When you looked around the church was jammers – even more packed than it was for Communions – and you saw loads of people from your school, including your teacher. You waved at her and she nodded at you.

'Turn around in your seat and face the altar,' your da said.

The baby's coffin was on a small stand at the end of the pew and it looked like a strange ornament sitting there. Someone had put a bouquet of yellow roses on top of it. Those are your ma's favourite, so maybe it was her. But then you didn't think it could have been, because she was in bits and she couldn't do anything any more.

You can't really remember much of the Mass; it's like as if you weren't really there. The choir sang some lovely songs, but they seemed far away, up on the balcony, and you don't know what most of the songs were. At the end, all the grown-ups were crying – your ma most of all, but your da held her by the elbow and that seemed to make her feel a bit stronger. The graveyard was the worst part because that was when you had to leave the baby forever and there wasn't even a headstone and you were afraid that everyone would forget where he was buried.

'There's no fear of that,' your da said and squeezed your hand. He said that it would take a while to get the grave set up right and that maybe your ma would let you help with picking the gravestone. You liked the sound of that.

'A carved angel would look nice,' you said, and your da said 'Indeed and it would.'

It was hot and still in the graveyard; there was another funeral on, but they all turned and looked at you because they knew yours was a child's funeral and that's the saddest type of all.

Afterwards your ma said that no one was allowed to come back to your house; she couldn't face another minute of it. So the black car brought you home, including your da, and the house was so dark and empty when you went inside. Your da put your ma up to bed and she was sobbing really loud and shouting that it wasn't fair. Your da said, 'I know, I know'. You didn't know what to do with yourself. Normally when you needed to think, you'd go down by the river but that seemed like a bad idea, so you stayed where you were. There was nothing to do and you didn't feel like doing anything anyway. You just made some scrambled eggs for you and Liam, because your da was still minding your ma, but the two of you only picked at them.

You could hear kids playing skipping on the street; somewhere up the valley a chainsaw was burring, cutting trees into logs. Car horns were beeping and it was as if it was any other normal day. You brought Liam up the stairs and the two of you got into bed in your clothes. Your da must have left when you were all asleep, because when you got up, he was gone.

3

Back to the River

The Olympics are on in Moscow. It's great the way everyone in the world gets to send a few people off to do all the different sports in the competitions. Except the Americans. They're boycotting the games. Like Captain Boycott in County Mayo, who charged too much rent so no one would talk to him or give him food or play sports with him or anything like that. You would love to be like Nadia Comăneci, who is excellent at gymnastics, but all you can do is a forward roll and a cartwheel where your legs won't go straight. You can do headstands on the sofa and on the floor, but only against the wall. Your da says the trick is balance, but that's easier said than done. He tries to do a headstand on a cushion in the middle of the floor but he falls over. Liam bursts out laughing and everyone stops and stares at him – glad he's happy – before laughing themselves. Then your da does it again, but Liam doesn't laugh the second time. Your da says that Nadia Comăneci has lovely legs, God bless her, and Geraldine gets offended because she's so fat at the moment.

Your da says he'll send you and Liam to gymnastics classes if you like and then maybe some day you'll be in the Olympics yourselves. You'd be very proud to win a medal for Ireland and your ma would be proud too. But you're afraid that all the other kids at the gymnastics class would be brilliant already, so you say that you won't bother going, but you hope that your da books you in anyway, as a surprise.

'We'll have to go over to the house and get you some clothes,' your da says to you. 'You haven't got enough of anything with you.'

'Will we see Mammy?' Liam whispers; he's never in the mood for talking any more.

'Mammy's gone to the hospital for a rest,' your da says and he picks Liam up and gives him a hug. Your da gives good hugs these days. 'But you can get some of your toys and books at the house and bring them back here and we'll play with them together.'

'And with Mammy,' Liam mumbles into your da's hair, and he looks at you across the top of Liam's head. His look is sad.

It takes two buses to get over from your da's flat to your house, and two buses to get back. Clare and Geraldine stay at home, thank God. Both of them are driving you nuts. You thought your ma was a moan until you met Geraldine; you don't know how your da sticks her. And as for Clare! She is the spoiledest brat on the planet and you would love to give her a hard slap. Even your da thinks she's a bit much sometimes, the way she carries on; you can tell. You'll have to hide any stuff you bring back, because Clare will only want it and Geraldine will think she should have it. She gives Clare absolutely everything she wants and says it's for the quiet life, but in your opinion Clare's never quiet.

It's great being on the bus with your da. You let Liam sit beside him, even though you would like to, but he turns in his seat to talk to you anyway. He points out things to you, like the army barracks where he was once a soldier and the church where he and your ma got married. It's a huge one with three holy statues sitting on the top, but they're so far up that you can't tell who they are. Your da says their wedding day was marvellous altogether and your ma looked stunning, as usual. He says he couldn't believe his luck that day. Then he goes quiet for a while. You don't mind because, in a way, you're feeling weird about seeing your own house. You just want to think to yourself and look out the window at the trees in the Phoenix Park rolling by.

You miss the baby's teeth. They were small and close together and in a little row in his mouth. Mostly when he smiled you couldn't see his teeth, but he had a special slow smile that pulled his top lip back a bit and you could see them then. His teeth looked extra supersonic white because they were new and because of his brown skin. They were beautiful. You don't allow yourself to think about him much, only in little snatches now and then, and you try to remember the good things. Not the day by the river, or the funeral, or the fact that he's in a grave now, small and completely by himself.

There are even worse things to think about. Like the worms getting in on him and crawling over his skin. Your da says that they won't be able to get into the coffin; worms can't chew through wood, thank God. Some nights you even think you might see the baby as a ghost in your room; when you get up for the toilet, you beg him not to appear to you. Even though you'd love to see him and give him a hug, you want to see him the way he used to be, not as a ghost.

In the night-time, in your da's flat, you miss the sounds of home. The flat has different sounds: the fridge shudders and rumbles and the pipes are always creaking because the heat's never turned off. There's something bigger missing as well and it took you a while to realise that it's the sound of the river. Your da's flat is high up and, apart from the aeroplanes passing over, all you can hear are muffled traffic noises and the people in the other flats moving around. You can hear their light switches and their hoovers and their tellies and their shouting. But there are no sounds of nature: no river, no rustly trees, no far-off cow mooing, and definitely no birds singing. The noises that you hear in the flat are so wrong to your ears that they make you feel closed in and afraid.

Your ma went off her head. She was drinking all the time and talking to herself out loud. She wouldn't have a bath or even eat anything, no matter what you made. She kept holding on to Liam and he didn't want to be held so much. You'd see him wriggling to get away from her, but she'd grip him and say he wasn't to go outside the door.

'Don't dare set foot by that river. Either of you,' she'd say.

One morning when you got up, she was sitting on the kitchen windowsill with her legs hanging out over the edge, over the river. She was throwing all the baby's clothes and toys into the water, one by one. You ran down to Cora and Noel's to get help. You banged at the door but they weren't there. Then you had to run all the way to the shop. Mrs Concannon let you use her phone, which is in the back, to ring your auntie Bridget.

Mrs Concannon normally hates kids; she says she hasn't got all day when you have only walked in the door and haven't even looked at the sweets yet. Then you're under pressure to choose your goodies quickly. That always confuses you and you end up picking the wrong thing. But she's nice to you now because of the tragedy in your family. She lifts aside the beady curtains to let you into the back room and they click and sway behind you. The room smells like cabbage. You're glad you know your auntie Bridget's phone number off by heart, but your hands are wobbling and you keep making mistakes dialling the number. In the end Mrs Concannon comes swishing through the curtains and gets you to call it out to her, and she does the dialling for you.

'Your aunt is busy; she can't come over,' she says, after talking for a minute on the phone and clumping the receiver back down real hard. 'Who else can you ring?'

You ask her if she knows the number of Kearney's butcher's shop in the village and she says indeed and she does, and she dials the number. Then she hands you the receiver and goes back out into her shop to serve the customers.

'Kearney's.'

‘Hello. Can I speak to Kit Nugent, please?’

‘Just a sec.’ The woman at the other end shouts: ‘Kit, it’s for you. One of your mots!’ You hear people laughing.

‘Hello?’ says a man into the phone. Your voice leaves you for a minute.

‘Oh, Kit,’ you gasp eventually, and the next thing you’re breathing and sobbing into the receiver, and he’s telling you to calm down. You tell him that your ma’s acting mad and throwing everything into the river and he says he’ll be over in two shakes, and that you’re to go home and keep an eye on her.

‘Don’t let her do anything stupid,’ he says, and you think she is being stupid enough already, what else could she do? But you run home and by the time you get there Liam’s up and he’s watching your ma throw the cushions off the sofa down into the water. They float away like boats, along with the tablecloth and the teddies and the baby’s clothes. She’s breathing hard through her nose, but when she turns to look at you her eyes are flat and glassed over. Then she makes her hands into fists and starts swiping at the air. Liam topples back away from her.

‘Ma, why don’t you lie down for a while?’ She nods yes, so you guide her up the stairs and settle her into her bed. You pet her hair and she closes her eyes. By the time Kit comes, she’s asleep, but the stuff’s gone forever into the river and it’s obvious that your ma’s not well at all. Kit says he will call the doctor and that he’ll stay with you and Liam, and that you’re not to worry about a thing. You stare at him and your neck feels choky, but you don’t want to cry in front of him. Or Liam.

‘Come on, Little Miss Prim,’ Kit says, ‘everything will be alright.’

He ruffles Liam’s hair and leaves the house to ring the doctor. After a while an ambulance comes. You look at Kit and he tells you that it’s for the best; that the doctor wouldn’t be able to give her the help she needs. He tells you that your da’s on his way over and that he’ll be able to say what will happen next.

Your da tips you on the shoulder and says it's time to get off the bus. The three of you walk in silence down the road. The house has a lonely look, like an old person's house that never gets done up. All the curtains and blinds are drawn and the small strip of garden at the front is gone weedy. Your ma normally keeps it lovely and neat.

'Don't give me house plants,' she always says. 'I'll only murder them on you. But give me an outside garden any day and I'll keep it nice for you.'

Your da opens the front door with his key and you swallow damp air as you move through the hall. The house is stiller than still. And it's dark.

'Right,' your da says and you nearly fall out of your skin. You were so busy feeling your way back into the house that you forgot he was with you. 'Let's air the place out a bit.'

So you go from room to room opening the curtains and blinds, and unhitching the clips from the windows before pushing them up. When you open the kitchen window, you gulp in the smell from the river, pulling it up through your nose and into your mouth. That feels good.

In your bedroom you run your finger through the coating of fluffy dust that's all over everything on the dressing table. There's a darkness in the room that you don't like and a sour smell. It's gloomy, like a room in a scary film. So you turn on the light and shove the window open and start singing like a maniac to make yourself feel different, more alive. It works.

Your da comes running up the stairs; he thinks there's something wrong and that you are crying or screaming or something. But when he sees you dusting things down with a pair of knickers – because that's all you can find – he starts laughing.

You flick the knickers at his head. 'Get on with it,' you say, and he goes to air out your ma's room.

You choose some shorts and your green skirt with the white rope belt and your broderie anglaise blouse and you stuff them all into a plastic bag. You bring the Sindy dolls as well, just in case you get really bored some day. You put in *Fear of Flying* too, for a little read, but you hide that at the bottom of the bag so that your da doesn't see. He would have a freak attack if he thought you were reading it. You go to Liam's room and put some clothes in a bag for him. He's standing there like a zombie, staring into the chest of drawers. You pick out toys and a few Ladybird books for him and lead him out onto the landing. Sometimes you feel sorry for him, but other times he's just a pain the way he mopes around. You always have to pull and drag him to do anything and it's making you tired and fed up.

'Right so, have you got everything?' your da says and you nod. 'We'll go down and see Cora and then we'll come back and close the windows. That'll get a bit of air through the place.'

Some of the kids from the street are playing around outside when you come out into the sunshine. They all stop what they are doing and stand and gawk at you. You know every single one of them, but only one girl says hello. You say hello back, but you feel like you're from another planet now and that they're right to stare at you. Your da guides you and Liam onto the path that leads to Cora's house. The river sighs behind you.

4

Another Letter

Gwen's letter is long, for her. It's the one Cora brought over and it's on lemon-coloured paper that makes a rustly noise when you unfold it. You sit on a stool out on the balcony, in the sun, to read it. All you can hear is the traffic far below and the sound of the breeze rasping against the sheets of paper in your hand. Sinbad licks at your toes; he likes the taste of feet. Gwen says she misses you. She says that her mam said that you can come to Wales and stay whenever you want. Her letter is full of happiness and joy, and it's obvious to you that she hasn't heard about the baby yet. You'll be very sorry to tell her, because people hate bad news and sometimes they shoot the messenger, which means they blame you for the bad news, as if it's all your fault. Even though you're only telling them.

You hope that the baby drowning is not your fault. You left him on the riverbank with Liam and Noel and Rory. They were in charge of him. Well, not Liam; he's too small. But really, you think that you should've stayed to mind the baby; your ma was relying on you. You should've sat there and not taken your eyes off him, to make sure he didn't toddle away and fall into the river when no one was looking. But how can you be to blame if Rory and Noel were playing cards when they were meant to have been keeping an eye? Your da says it's no one's fault, that it's just a terrible, terrible tragedy that never should have taken place. He says no one knows why these things happen, but that God must've wanted the baby to be with him in heaven, to keep him company.

'Yeah, but I don't believe in God,' you say. Your da looks at you funny, but he doesn't pass any comment. 'Anyway, God has enough angels up there. Why does he have to take our baby and make us all so sad?'

Your da gives you a hug and says he doesn't know. 'Life's not fair most of the time, I'm sorry to have to tell you,' he says.

Geraldine gives you a notepad to write back to Gwen on, because you forgot to bring your box of fancy paper from home. The notepad's blue and has lines, which is helpful when you're trying to do your best writing. It's very hard to know what to say to Gwen when she's going on about swimming in a pool and her new friend Olive – who you're glad to hear she's fighting with, so they're not really great friends any more – and all about her new house and garden. Gwen has a den in the house in Wales, which is the American name for a playroom, and all her stuff's in there, including a portable telly all for herself. It sounds deadly.

You chew your pencil until the wood on the top gets soggy and flakes of orange paint get stuck to your tongue. You have to go inside and look in the mirror to scrape them all off. In the end you write that you are so sorry to break the very bad news that your baby brother has drowned, and that you and Liam have had to move in with your da because your ma's resting in the hospital. You tell Gwen all about Sinbad and the girls who broke the bottle of milk. Then, to make the letter a bit happier, you describe the day out you had in Dún Laoghaire with Cora and Noel; how you saw the ferries that go to Wales and you thought about her. Then you put 'Yours sincerely' and Geraldine says she'll post it for you when she goes to the shops for the messages. You go back out onto the balcony to look at the haze that's hanging over the roads; the sun causes it.

You can hear Geraldine talking. Sometimes she's so ordinary and nice, but mostly she's tired and cranky. Her and your da don't see eye to eye over Liam. You listen harder. Geraldine says that it's not normal the way Liam refuses to talk, but your da says it's only natural, considering what he's been through. He says he's obviously missing his mammy.

'Well, I've no intention of being his mother,' Geraldine says, 'I've enough on my plate.'

'I didn't ask you to be,' your da murmurs.

'Well they're here, aren't they?'

'Keep your voice down.'

'Well, all I want to know is, when is Joan taking them back? They can't stay with us forever, you know. We have our own family to think of.'

You can just imagine her rubbing her big old belly when she says that. As if she's rubbing the baby itself, instead of just the skin of her stomach. Her baby. You don't even care that the new baby will be a relative of yours. It doesn't feel like it. You're glad that Liam's in the bedroom looking at his comics and not listening to Geraldine going on real spiteful. You decide that you'll get in touch with Cora, so that you can go and see your ma. She'll have to leave that hospital and take you home. She can't be all that bad; it's not like she's dying or anything.

Geraldine comes out on the balcony and stands beside you, looking down. The front of her dress is swollen and she stands with her feet wide apart. She leans on the railing and sighs. You get a whiff of her lemony smell; it's nice and fresh. She lifts a handful of your hair and lets it fall back against your shoulders.

'We'll have to get a bit cut off this,' she says, 'just a smidgin.'

She pats you on the head. You're not sure. Your ma always cuts your hair and you don't really want Geraldine hacking away at it. But then she says she'll bring you over to her friend Róisín, who is a hairdresser, and you change your mind completely. You've never had a proper haircut before. Hair salons are lovely, full of fancy shampoo and posh ladies and millions of mirrors. Like Mrs Brabazon's place.

'I'll go and give her a bell and see when she can fit you in.' She waddles back inside.

You go to the balcony door and look into the flat. It's like the inside of a cave it's so dark, but your eyes get used to it after a minute. You watch Geraldine go over to the phone and you think maybe she's not so bad.

It turns out Róisín doesn't have her own hairdressing salon at all. She cuts people's hair in her house. But she's lovely; she's always laughing.

'So this is Willy's little one,' she says, when she opens the door to let you into her house.

'That's right,' Geraldine says.

'Well, isn't she only gorgeous?' You go scarlet, but you think that Róisín's a very nice person. 'Well, she obviously looks like her mother; there isn't a trace of Willy in her. Except for the hair, maybe!' Róisín laughs, as if she's made a funny joke, and she hugs you, but you only smile. 'Anyway, we'll do something fab with this hair and you'll be even more gorgeous than you are now.'

She has one of those sinks in the shape of a collar and she sits you down and makes you lie back into it while she washes your hair. Her hands are firm on your head, but it doesn't hurt. Meanwhile, though, your neck's breaking in the collar-sink. You don't say anything because you don't want to make her feel bad. She has the radio turned up and, in between talking to Geraldine, she sings along to the songs in a happy way. You're glad when she finishes washing your hair. She dabs at your head with a towel and squidges all the water out of the ends, into the sink.

'Now, pet, sit over here and we'll comb you out,' Róisín says, and then she asks Geraldine about the baby and what names she's come up with and whether she thinks it'll be a boy or a girl. Geraldine says she doesn't mind as long as it's healthy and she smiles. She's like a different person when she's away from the flat and Clare, and all the worry of everything.

Róisín uses a comb with big wide teeth on your hair and keeps stopping to ask if she's hurting you. You shake your head even though she sometimes drags on a knot and it's sore. Her house is lovely. She has curtains with black and red designs and a tablecloth to match. The sun beams through the window and shines across the lino and you can see the dust dancing like a band of happy flies. Not that Róisín's house is dirty; there are normal amounts of dust.

'I think we'll give her a pageboy, Ger, what do you think? With a fringe and all.'

Geraldine nods from behind the *Woman's Way* she's reading and Róisín starts clacking with the scissors. She's singing and clicking and laughing; you watch big clumps of wet hair falling all around you. Next thing she has a huge hairdryer and she rolls your hair around a bristly brush and you watch yourself being transformed. Your hair's short and shiny and a fringe flops above your eyes, like a bird's wing. You don't even mind any more that your hair's the colour of toffee and not coal-dark like your ma's. You feel like a new person, someone clean and grown-up and special.

On the way back to the flat on the bus, you sit in the window seat, pretending to be watching what's outside, but really you're looking at your own reflection and admiring how different you are now. When you walk in to the sitting room, your da pretends that he doesn't know who you are, which is a bit babyish, but you're glad that he's noticed that you're a different person.

'Who's this?' he keeps saying and Liam thumps him and laughs, because he knows well that your da knows it's you.

'Well?' Geraldine says to your da. All her smiles are gone and instead she has a big narky lip-disappearing face. 'Did you ring her?'

'Not now, Ger,' your da says, but then he changes his mind because she stays standing there and she's obviously in a mood. He tells you and Liam to go on out to the balcony and play with Sinbad.

'You look thick with that hair,' Liam says, and runs out onto the balcony before you can hop on him and give him a nuggy to the head.

'Not half as thick as you!' you shout, running after him.

You leave the balcony door open a little and listen to your da and Geraldine. They're not exactly fighting, but you can hear the tears soaking through Geraldine's voice. You can't hear much of what they're saying, so you move your eye to the slit and peep through, sliding the door wider to listen better.

'All I want is a bit of peace and quiet in my own home. Is that too much to ask for?'

'No, no,' your da says, putting his arm around her. 'It's just that Cora said Joan is still in a bad way. She said it wouldn't be a good idea for the kids to even see her at the moment. Maybe in a week or so.'

'Oh my God, I can't cope.'

'Look, she'll be well again soon. I'll go and see her myself and tell her that she'll have to take them back, that we just haven't the space. OK?'

'OK.'

You move back from the balcony door. Liam's kneeling down beside Sinbad, scratching the back of his knobbly grey fur. Sinbad's neck's thrown back and he's kind of grinning with his bottom teeth, making his happy face; really he looks kind of ugly and crazy. He makes grunty doggy noises and you think at least someone has a nice life; at least one creature in this world's having a happy time on earth, because you certainly aren't. You smell the hot air of the city, full of smoke and car-stink and greasiness. You miss the tree-noise and river-hush of home. You miss your ma and the baby so much that if you let yourself think about it for too long you'd probably choke to death. Sinbad pushes his wet nose into your hand looking for a treat. Greedy little piggy, you think. Two aeroplanes make cloudy slug-tracks across the sky and their noise trails far behind them.

Your da doesn't want you and Liam any more.

5

A Plan and A Boat

It's no use telling Liam about the plan. He'll only blab. It won't be long until you'll be gone. You act cool towards your da, only giving him small answers when he talks to you, but he doesn't even notice. Geraldine's getting her bag ready for the hospital. She's folding up the little vests and cardigans and she lets you help. Her baby's nightdresses are soft and they close over with tiny ribbons. All the little clothes smell lovely, like cool morning air. You remember when your ma was doing this, getting ready for the baby. You ask Geraldine for a stamp.

'More letters?' she says, raising her eyebrows like two pointy hills, and you nod. She gives you one from her purse and you write another letter to Gwen, a short one this time. You drag Sinbad down the stairs for a walk and run down to the shops to post the letter yourself. On the way back you dawdle. It's hard to think in the flat, with Clare banging her Lego and Liam glued to the noise of the telly. And Geraldine always wants you to help with something: packing bags or washing the delft or sweeping the floor. She treats you like some kind of servant. She doesn't boss you around much when your da's there; she pretends like you are best buddies when he's at home. You'll show her and it'll serve her right.

Sinbad scuffles along, sniffing at the ground and lifting his leg every five seconds. You drag at him; that makes him pull against the lead and bump his bum along the path, but really you're in no hurry. He does more piddles and more smelling, hugging himself close to the walls in case he misses a drop of some other dog's pee-pee. He's disgusting.

Your new hairstyle will be an advantage, you think. There's no photo of you with pageboy hair, so people won't be able to identify you. If only you could get Liam to dress like a girl, then you'd be exactly like Finn and Derval Dove in *The Flight of the Doves*. Only in reverse. That's one of your favourite books of all time. They even made a film of it. No one would want to make a film of you. Then you think that on second thoughts, there's no point trying to put a dress on Liam; nothing of yours would fit him and where are you supposed to get a wig, anyway? He'll have to do as he is.

You'll need plenty of money. You're sorry to rob from your da, but you have no choice. Anyway, his tin in the wardrobe's packed full of money and there's no way he'll miss a few pounds. You'll need bus fares and money for food. And a present for Gwen. And one for her mam. You'll pretend it's from your da, so that she won't ask any questions. When you were in Dún Laoghaire with Cora and Noel, you saw how you can bunk onto the ferry. It's simple. When no one's looking, you'll get into the back of a van or a truck and hide. Then when it drives up the ramp and into the belly of the boat you'll get out. But not until the ferry's out in the harbour a bit. Then there'll be no turning back.

Your da and Geraldine are going into town to buy a go-car for the new baby. Geraldine doesn't like the real big prams, so she's getting a special go-car with a seat that can lie back; it will do the new baby until he's big. It costs a fortune, but she says it'll be worth it, because she'd be killed trying to get a proper pram up and down the stairs if the lift was broken. Clare's going with them into town. It'll be a relief to get away from her; she cries like an ambulance siren all day: *wee-wah, wee-wah, wee-wah*. It drives you baloobas and you have to hide in the loo sometimes to read in peace or just to hear the thoughts in your head.

Everything's ready. After breakfast you wave at the three of them from the balcony to make sure they're gone. It takes them ages to disappear; Geraldine walks very slow because of her heavy belly. You've to drag Liam away from the telly to tell him the plan. First of all he gawps at you and scratches his ear. Then he half-smiles and nods. Next thing he's laughing like a madser and hopping around on one foot. You get him to calm down and take his toothbrush from the bathroom. You have packed everything into your two schoolbags. They still smell like wet and old lunch, even though they've been empty for weeks. You give Sinbad a little nuggy-pet on the head and then lock him out on the balcony. He looks at you through the glass door with question marks in his eyes.

Last thing is the money. You go into your da's room and creak open the wardrobe. The tin's where it always is, under a pile of vests. You're hot and your breath's hard to get out when you pop the lid. You can't believe it. There's hardly anything left in the tin, just a few damp notes. He must've taken all the money to pay for the bloody go-car. You have to take what's left, but you promise yourself that some day you'll pay it back to your da, cross your heart and hope to die.

You end up having to buy tickets for the boat.

'Where's your mammy and daddy?' your man says, stretching out of his cabinet to look over your head. There's a drippy bit on the end of his nose; you can't help staring at it. You have the lie ready; you point to the queue of people waiting to get on the boat.

'That's our mammy, in the red trousers. She said I could come over and buy our tickets because I'm big now. She already got hers.' You look him straight in the eye.

'I see,' he says, making a sniff with his mouth. Then he mutters about people putting on airs and graces, but you have the tickets, so you don't give a flying fig roll what he says or thinks. Now nearly all the money is gone, but you'd no choice, because the trucks and cars were already on the ferry by the time you arrived in Dún Laoghaire. You never thought of that.

You swallow the taste of burning oil that hangs over the air on the deck. It's really noisy, between all the people and the engines and the hundreds of seagulls that are screeching around overhead. Liam holds his hands over his ears. You pull him back from the railings where everyone's gathered waiting for the ferry to pull away, so they can wave goodbye to Ireland. You don't want people seeing you from the pier.

It's another lovely day, but the breeze makes it feel cold. The lady in the red trousers, from the queue, is sitting on a blue chair that's nailed to the deck, with her face held up to the sun. She has a plastic scarf covering her hair and she wears brown sunglasses, like the ones a film star would have. Seeing her close up, you think she's probably too old to be yours and Liam's ma. She lifts her sunglasses and fixes her eyes on you. With her other hand she sends you a tiny wave. You turn away and drag Liam through all the people and their sticky-out elbows to the other side of the deck, the part that faces the sea. The boat shudders under you and glides away from the pier in slow motion. You follow the railing around and look down at the grey water sloshing against the sides of the ferry; it's carrying bottles and paper and other rubbish. It makes you think of the brownness of the river beside the house, your river, with its floating logs and weed-clumps. Steering Liam farther along the railings to see the lifeboats that are tied up, you suck the fishy smell of the sea through your nose. You think it's funny how water can have different smells.

Now you're back to the part of the deck where you started from. The lady in the red trousers pats the blue seat beside her. You look behind you to see if she means someone else, even though you know it's you she's calling. Taking Liam by the shoulders, you push him through the crowd to where she's sitting.

The lady shades her eyes with her hand. Her sunglasses are propped on her head, over the see-through headscarf. She winks at you.

'Are you kiddies all alone?'

You don't answer. She seems so nice that it'd be mean to lie to her. Then you shake your head a little.

'Oh, I see,' she says. 'Well, I *am* all alone, so why don't you keep me company here for a bit?' You shuffle Liam forward into a seat and then you sit yourself. You feel stiff. Every so often you glance sideways at the lady, but she has covered up her eyes with the sunglasses again. Liam bursts out laughing.

'Something's funny, eh?' says the lady. Then she laughs herself because the ferry lets a long loud belchy noise that gives everyone a fright. When all that's left of the sound is a dancing in your ears, she introduces herself. 'I'm Bella. Bella Larkin.' She gives each of you her hand to shake. It feels squashy, like one of those yellow sponges for wiping up mess in the kitchen.

Liam says 'Bella-wella-fella' and starts laughing again, but you give him a thump.

'Hey!' he roars, rubbing at his arm. You hardly tipped him. Your ma would murder him if she heard him being so rude to an old lady. Bella Larkin's hair is orange. It's a mad colour – it looks like Lucozade – but she must think it's lovely. It stands in solid peaks under her plastic headscarf. Your eyes get glued to it; even the wind can't make her hair move.

'Would you like a sweetie, dearie?' she says and holds out a brown paper bag.

You're not allowed to take sweets from anyone; it's a definite rule, even if the person seems nice. It's because of what happened to your ma when she was around your age. She went to see a film by herself (she wasn't supposed to) and a man offered her a sweet. But when she put her hand into the bag on his lap, there was something alive in there instead. Your ma always gets a bit scarlet when she tells you about that. But you know it's a warning and that she'd string you up if you ever took sweets from anyone.

'No thanks,' you say, not even looking at Bella Larkin. But after a minute you see that Liam is chomping away on a liquorice allsort, the black stuff streeling down his chin. You love allsorts. 'Well, maybe just one.' She hands over the whole bag.

'Take a few, poppet.'

It's not nice to be greedy, so you take two: a big one with black, brown and white layers, and a roundy pink one that has a small tubey bit of liquorice down the middle. It's your favourite one of the lot; it has coconut in it. The three of you sit there, smelling the salty air and eating sweets. You wish Anne Brabazon could see you. She wouldn't be so great with all her poxy Irish dancing medals and her ma's fancy hair salon if she knew you were off on an adventure; off to see Gwen all by yourself. Well, by yourself except for Liam. Anyway, Anne would be mad jealous.

'Our ma is in the hos-dible,' Liam says and you give him daggers.

You'd warned him that if he was going to bother talking he'd better keep his trap shut about your life. You told him it was important to pretend not to be himself, or they'd come and send him back to Geraldine and your da and Clare the whinge-bag.

'Oh,' Bella says. 'My husband died in a hospital. Nasty places.'

Liam's face starts to crumple. 'Ma's not going to die, Liam. No way.' You put your arm around him. 'She's just having a rest until she feels a bit better and then she's coming out.'

'Oh, I am a silly old bat,' Bella says. 'I'm sorry, little man. I didn't mean to frighten you. My old Dan died a long time ago and he was really very, very sick. Sick the way only old people get. Your mummy will be right as rain in no time, I'm sure.'

Liam makes his bottom lip all blubbery, and you know when

he does that he's only pretending to be still upset. He eats another few of Bella's allsorts, stuffing two or three into his gob at the same time. You make a face at him to get him to slow down, but he bugs his eyes at you, which means 'Get lost'. You watch the gulls swooping and screeching in the sky around the boat, looking for things to eat. They're huge; they have plump bellies like the ducks on the river at home, and they're not afraid to come near people. Sometimes they look as if they'd poke your eye out with their big orange beaks.

Liam complains that he's cold. Bella says you should all go into the lounge, away from the wind and crowds; she stands up to go. Liam jumps up too. He's grinning at Bella, as if she's his long-lost granny or something. You were feeling OK, but now you're a bit afraid of the way she's bossing you around.

'No. We'll stay here.'

'I want to go inside,' Liam whines.

You pull him by the hand. 'Liam Dunne, I'm in charge and I said we're staying here.'

'Suit yourself, sweetie pie, but that brother of yours needs to be kept warm. That's all I'm saying.'

You're sorry then for being so narky. She's only making sure that Liam is alright and warm enough. And she's nice and very good at sharing.

'Well, maybe we'll go in for a little while.'

Liam holds the door open for you and Bella to go into the inside part of the ship. You heave through the door, the wind at your back, and a wave of warmness blows over you. The air smells sweet, like candyfloss, and you see rows of whirring slot machines along the corridor. You would love a go of one of them, but you know you have to save the little money that's left.

'Let's have a bit of brunch,' Bella says. 'My treat.'

'Brunch-munch-lunch,' Liam sings and takes Bella's hand in his.

She smiles down at him. The boat rocks, making your feet land in mid-air and then thump onto the carpet when you walk. You follow them into the restaurant, which is packed with people eating dinners, even though it's still morning.

You think to yourself that you're glad you and Liam met Bella Larkin.

6

A Visit

Your da brought you and Liam to see your ma; she was in a different hospital to the last time. It had all low little buildings, spread out from each other and painted fawn, which is the exact colour of banana ice cream. There were lots of grassy bits in the grounds, and benches and droopy-branched trees. Some of the patients were sitting out. It wasn't like a hospital at all, except for the smell when you went inside one of the buildings; it was clean and sharp, with dinner-hotness behind it. Even most of the doctors and nurses didn't look like they were supposed to look; they were wearing jeans and ordinary tops, instead of white coats and those things for listening to people's hearts. It was a good sign, you thought; the people in the hospital couldn't be very sick if they didn't need proper doctors and nurses.

At the end of a corridor you got to a gate and a window that were locked and your da had to ring the bell. You could hear some loony screaming; it sounded like they were banging their head off a radiator. It was ages before anyone came to the locked gate. The one who came was a big fatso; she looked like a Christmas pudding with legs.

'Yeah?'

'We're here to see Joan Dunne.'

Pudding Woman flicked through a book. 'Yeah, she's been moved. There was a bit of aggro here last night; we had to move a few of them.'

'What kind of aggro?' your da asked.

Pudding Woman looked at him as if to say 'Don't ask me my top-secret business, you nosy man', then slammed the book shut and put her hands on her hips. She made her eyes all slitty. 'Who did you say you were looking for again?'

'Joan Dunne.'

'Oh yeah. Dunne, Dunne, Dunne.' She had the book open again and spent ages going through it, sliding her chubby finger down the pages. 'Yeah, she's not here.'

Your da gritted his teeth. 'Well, *where* is she?'

'Hospital B,' your woman said, not even lifting her eyes.

You could see your da was going to ask her where Hospital B was, but then he changed his mind. 'Come on, kids,' he said instead.

It took you ages to find Hospital B because it turned out it hadn't been called that for years. You wandered from building to building, looking for a sign that said Hospital B, until eventually your da asked a man where it was; he didn't know. In the end he stopped an old woman.

'Sorry, excuse me, I'm looking for Hospital B?' he said, in his best telephone voice.

'You mean Hospital Two.'

'Ah, no. We're looking for Hospital B.'

'Hospital Two,' she said again, and she rubbed her hands across her boobs. You were scarlet for her, but seeing her doing that made Liam start giggling. Your da sighed and scratched his head.

'It used to be called "B" but now it's called "Two". Hospital Two.' She smiled and pointed to the building beside the one you thought your ma was living in in the first place. A nurse came over.

'Now, Kathleen, don't be bothering these nice people,' she said, and your da smiled at the old woman. She started doing a big hee-haw laugh like a donkey and felt her boobs again. The nurse guided her away; the old woman was one of the loonies.

Your ma was in Saint Philomena's wing. All the wings were called after saints and they each had a statue of their saint in a special hollowed-out cave above the door. You recognised Saint Philomena immediately because your granny had a great devotion to her (as well as to gazillions of other saints) when she was alive. She was one of the statues that lived on your granny's shelf and you always thought that Saint Philomena was gorgeous-looking; you wouldn't have minded being like her. She had big chocolate-button eyes and heaps of long black hair, and she carried arrows and palm fronds in her arms. Your granny's Philomena had a red cloak, but the one in the hospital wore a peach gown. She looked a bit different, but you still knew it was her. You felt a bit sorry for Philomena, though, because they un-sainted her after hundreds of years. You'd think they'd have just left her as she was. Your granny said it was all nonsense anyway, and that the powers that be in Rome had shot themselves in the foot, because people loved Philomena more than ever after they took her saintliness away.

You got to another one of the locked gates with a window; the Pudding Woman must have told them you were coming, because they were expecting you. The man in charge smiled and gave you and Liam a lollipop each. You're too big for lollipops, but it's the thought that counts. A man nurse brought you down all these corridors, past loads of closed doors. The air was as warm as a blanket and it was very quiet. He knocked on a door and opened it without waiting for an answer. There, sitting on one of the two beds, was your ma. She had her clothes on – a tracksuit – with a dressing-gown over it. Her face was gone as skinny as a skeleton and her hair was all over the place, but it was her, alright. She dragged her eyes up to look at you, but it was like as if she didn't even notice you all standing here. Liam hid behind your da. You went right into the room and stood beside her bed. She hung her head to the floor.

'Hello, Ma; it's us.' You petted her head with your fingers.

Your da said 'Joan', but she still didn't look up. Liam went and sat beside her on the bed.

'Now look what you did!' she snapped at him, smoothing out the bedspread real fast with her hand, wiping and pulling at it until it was flat again. Then she stopped and sat there on the bed, looking at nothing. Liam jumped up and ran behind your da. He told him it was alright, but Liam wouldn't let go of his leg, and when your da tried to pull him away, Liam said 'Fuck off', which gave everyone a shock. Except your ma, who slumped there like a sack of potatoes.

'Do you want to stay?' the man nurse said to your da in a bored voice, picking the dirt out of his fingernails and flicking it at the wall.

'Yes we do,' your da said, closing the door nearly in your man's face.

You put the grapes and lemonade and the 'Get Well Soon' cards that you and Liam had made on top of the locker. It was hard to know what to do next. Your ma was acting like a spacer from the planet Mars. It was as if some aliens had sucked out the parts of her that made her your ma and left nothing at all inside. Your da grunted and tried to peel Liam off his leg again; he was glued onto him.

Then Liam shot forward and started thumping your ma in the stomach, really belting her hard.

'I hate you! I hate you! I hate you!' he roared.

'Jesus, Mary and Joseph! Liam, stop that!' your da said, and dragged him off her.

Your ma didn't move or blink or do anything. You couldn't believe it. Then she lifted her head and looked at Liam as if she'd only noticed him. She shrugged and said 'I don't know,' even though none of you had asked her anything.

The quietness of the room buzzed in your brain; far away you heard someone shout, and a radio started singing out down the corridor. Sobs fell out of Liam. Your ma tucked her legs up and lay down on the bed. Your da nodded his head at the door, so you opened it and the three of you went out. He picked Liam up and carried him down the corridor, back the way you'd come only five minutes before. In another few minutes you were being dazzled by the sunshine and the traffic was screeching past on the road outside the hospital grounds. If only Saint Philomena could come alive and take care of your ma, you thought.

'We'll go and visit Cora while we're over this side of town,' your da said, and you thought that was a great idea. It was too soon to have to go back to Geraldine and Clare, who didn't want you in their home anyway.

It was lovely to walk across the bridge and down by the old stone wall to Cora's house. You pulled the river air up into your nose and your head. The wind was crowding through the trees, light and swishy, the way you liked it. Cora was thrilled to see you; it was all hugs and kisses and 'What a nice surprise' out of her.

'I'm a lady of leisure again,' she said, 'ould Mags Brabazon was giving me a pain in my backside, so I left the job!' You all laughed. 'So, Willy, anything strange or startling?' she said, pushing you all into her hall.

'We were up at Saint Jude's.'

'Oh, I see.' Cora rubbed her stiff fingers together like a crab pincing its claws. 'Hmmm. How was she?'

'Not good. Not good at all. I don't know what I was expecting. I was kind of hoping to talk to her, you know, about when she'd be home and that.'

'Well, not for a while, by the look of things. I was up with her on Wednesday myself.'

Cora lifted the kettle and told you to get the fizzy orange and biscuits from the press. She said to scoot off into the sitting room while she talked to your da. You went in and turned on the telly and drank the orange, letting the fizz attack your tongue before you swallowed it. Cora and Noel's house is great the way it's always full of goodies. That's one of the things you like about it; a thing you don't like is the smell: smoked cigarettes and damp, always the same. But you don't blame Cora for that any more; you know it's just because it's an old house and that being near the river causes all sorts of wetness to gather in the air and make a stink.

Noel came in after a while. 'Be the hokey,' he said, 'would you look what the cat dragged in?'

'Noel!' Liam threw himself across the room.

'You don't *have* a cat,' you said, but you smiled to let him know that you were only messing too. Liam squashed onto the armchair beside Noel.

'So how's life in flatland?' Noel scratched his belly and it was so big it reminded you of Geraldine. The baby made her all roundy, but with Noel it was probably too many of Cora's ginormous dinners. He turned to Liam. 'Has that cat got your tongue? Has he? Did Cora's new cat bite out your tongue and swally it up?' Noel winked at you and tiddled Liam.

'He's kind of stopped talking since, well, since you know...' Noel nodded and his face creased back on itself. He pulled his fingers across his chin and you could see the coal-dirt in every crease of his skin. He didn't say anything. 'Geraldine doesn't like us,' you said.

'Ah now, what's that supposed to mean?' Noel leaned towards you and you edged onto the front of the sofa.

'She says she has to make stew for dinner because we're there. She says we're picky. We're not, *she* just doesn't like stew, but she takes it out on us. She slops it into the bowls real rough and bits of the juice spill onto the table and onto us. Scalding us. She does it on purpose.'

'Well, now.'

'And she's always picking on Liam. She goes mental at him, even when he's done nothing. She calls him names. I heard her.'

'You couldn't have that,' Noel said.

'And da lets her.'

'I hate Geraldine,' Liam said, jumping up and down on the arm of Noel's chair.

Cora came in. 'Stop that trick-acting, Liam,' she said, but not in an angry way. 'Come in the lot of you now and have a bit of dinner.'

'It's probably stew, is it, Cora?' said Noel, winking at you.

'Sure who'd make stew in this heat?' said Cora, sweeping you all into the kitchen. 'I did a few rashers and sausages and eggs. Kit brought me down some lovely pork sausages last night.'

'Kit,' said Liam, looking up at Cora, but that was all.

Noel was quiet at the dinner table, but Cora's good at yakking on and she did enough talking for everyone. You wondered if Kit had ever gone up to Saint Jude's to see your ma, but you didn't want to ask.

7

Bella Larkin

Bella say her name means 'beautiful lady'. You would love a name like that. It suits her, you think, even if her skin's wrinkly like a stale apple and her hair's blazing orange. She was probably lovely-looking when she was young, but she still looks smart in her red trousers and white mac. Bella confides in you that her real name's Bernadette, but only her Father ever called her that and he's six feet under since the year dot. Bella says the men in her life were all Irish, so it's no big surprise that she ended up staying there even after her old Dan passed away.

'But I'm as Welsh as a daffodil, just like my mam was,' she says, with a happy laugh.

You're having jelly and ice cream to finish off a lovely dinner of chicken and roast potatoes and gravy. It's like as if it's Sunday, only you're not at home with your ma and the baby; instead you're sailing across the Irish Sea to your new life. But you'll see your ma again; it's not as if you've forgotten about her or anything like that. Liam's slurping the jelly through his teeth, the way he does at home, and you have to tell him to behave himself. But Bella doesn't seem to mind. She says it's like having a lovely day out with the grandchildren she never had.

'We have no grannies,' says Liam.

'Neither do I, little man. Why don't we take a turn around the deck?' says Bella, pushing back her chair. 'We must be halfway across the sea by now.'

'Deadly,' Liam says.

You all troop outside and a blast of wind gusts your skirt up; you have to hold it down with your hands.

'Oh my, it's very fresh!' Bella says.

There are lots of people on the deck, being blown about and laughing at each other when their hair blows straight up in the air or when they have to fight against the wind to even walk. The three of you make your way to the back of the boat to watch the churn of white waves that the ferry drags behind it. It leaves a long frothy trail in the blue-green water that probably reaches all the way back to Ireland. The gulls are dipping down into it, snatching at the sea.

'The boat is leaving lots of nice titbits for them,' Bella says.

'Titbits, bitbits, sitbits,' Liam says, and Bella calls him a little rascal.

She turns to you. 'So,' she says.

You look away. 'So, what?'

'Well, you know as well as I do that you two should have someone with you, taking care of you.' She says nothing for a minute. 'Liam is very young.'

'I'm six!' Liam shouts and Bella gives him a sideways hug. She looks at you again.

'We've been invited to stay with Gwen, my friend.'

'And where does this Gwen live?' You don't answer; the wind fiddles with your hair, swishing it into your eyes. 'She's meeting you, is she? Off the ferry?' You look out at the water, turning and jumping behind the boat like a wild dolphin. Bella sighs. 'What am I supposed to do?'

'You don't have to do anything.'

'But I feel responsible for you, sweetheart. For you and Liam.' The wind whips at her plastic headscarf and she holds it down with her hand.

'Well, you needn't.' All of a sudden you feel like crying. It's all Bella Larkin's fault.

'Don't cry, sweetie pie. Let's go and sit somewhere and you can tell me all about it.'

Bella guides you back towards the door and to the inside of the boat; you sit down in a corner of the Shamrock Bar. She gives Liam some change and tells him to have a few tries on the slot machines. You end up telling her everything and you're crying like a maniac. You tell her all about Kit and your ma; you tell her about how the baby fell into the river when you weren't there to mind him; about Jonah, the baby's daddy; about your da and Geraldine and how she hates you and especially Liam; about your half-sister, Clare, and the new baby that's coming; about Cora and Noel, who are so nice, but Noel's partly to blame for the baby drowning; about your cousin Rory; about your ma being in the hospital for loony-tunes, acting as if she couldn't see you when you went to visit; and about Gwen, and how her mam said you were welcome to come and stay in Wales any time you wanted.

Bella hands you tissues. When you are finished talking, she says 'Oh dear.' You get the hiccups in the middle of it all, so she gets you some 7UP from the bar to take them away. The bubbles in the drink only makes them worse and you laugh, even though you are full of snots and tears and burpy hiccups. She takes your hands in her soft ones and says everything will be fine. She's so kind that you believe her. She asks if you have Gwen's letter with you, so you take it out of your schoolbag and show it to her.

'I take it they're not expecting you,' she says after reading it. You shake your head. 'Well, I can make sure that you get there safely at least.' Big tears drop out of your eyes into your lap and Bella puts her arms around you. A huge hiccup jumps through your body and the two of you burst out laughing. 'Let's have a nice cup of tea,' she says, and you drink tea with her though you have been off it for years. You gulp it and it's scalding, but it makes your belly feel comfy and warm.

The rest of the ferry journey is calm but your eyes are achy from all the bawling. Bella helps you to change your money from Irish pounds to English pounds; they have a tiny bank on the boat. Wales doesn't have a money all of its own; they use the English stuff. It has pictures of the Queen on it, wearing her crown and looking snooty. It doesn't take long for the three of you to gather up your stuff when the boat stops and get on the bus that'll bring you to 12 Penarth Walk, Bangor, which is where Gwen lives. Your legs feel all sway-ey when you get back on to dry land.

Wales is very green. They have grass and trees and mountains. That surprises you. You thought that only Ireland was like that; everyone calls it the Emerald Isle and says that the green there is in forty different shades. You didn't think that anyone else had the same colours of green that Ireland has, but they're here in Welsh Wales. That's what Bella calls it. Liam calls it 'Whales', like the mammal, but he also calls 'Weetabix' 'Wheetabix' so it's not very surprising. You get fed up correcting him, so you just let him say Whales if he wants to.

Bella's going to stay with her sister in Llandudno, but she's bringing you and Liam to Gwen's place on the way. She's full of facts. She tells you that the bit of land that Holyhead is on, where the boat leaves you, is an island called Anglesey. Bella says that the village with the longest place name in Britain is on the island and it's called Llanfairpwllgwyngyllgogerychwyrndrobwllllantysilio-gogogoch. She tries to teach you how to say it but all you can remember are the start and the end. You get her to say it over and over and you and Liam are in stitches laughing at the sound of it rolling out of her mouth. It's hard to say and it shows how clever Bella is that she can rhyme it off no bother. She says it means 'the church by the whirlpool and the red cave' or something like that; she can't exactly remember. She tells you that people call it Llanfair PG for short and that, for such a long name, it's a really tiny place, with only a train station and one shop. You think that's amazing. The longest place name in Ireland is Newtownmountkennedy and that's not half as long or half as hard to say.

Wales whizzes past the bus-window while Bella tells you all about it. Liam falls asleep between the two of you, and your head's nodding into sleep when Bella says it's time to get off. A cold wind seeps through your body when you step off the bus. It wakes you right up. Bella tells a taxi man she wants to go to Penarth Walk and back again, and he says that'll be fine. The three of you huddle in the back of the car and Bella scribbles her sister's number in Llandudno on a piece of paper, as well as her own address and phone number in Ireland.

'In case you need me, lovey,' she says, pushing it into your hand.

Bangor looks nice. You see a big church that reaches high into the sky and you have a quick prayer-thought for your ma. The car pulls up at the end of a road of stone-fronted houses that's swaying with trees. Bella gets out with you and gives you each a kiss on the cheek. She tells you to run along and you walk backwards away from her before turning to check the numbers of the houses. You go up the steps to the front door of number twelve and ring the bell; you hear it ding-dong through the house. The door opens. You look back down the road and Bella's still there; she sends you a little wave, hops into the taxi, and then she's gone.

'Good God almighty,' Gwen's mam says, her mouth making a shocked 'o', and she calls out for her husband to come to the door.

Sometimes when you think about yourself, you're one way, and sometimes you're a different way. It's easy to like yourself on some days and easy to hate yourself on others. It depends on your mood, or how many silly things you've said and done in that day. It's the same with other people: sometimes they seem to hate you and sometimes they seem to like you, depending on how you act. Normally Gwen's mam doesn't like you; she pretends that she does, for Gwen's sake, but you can see through her like a sheet of glass. Your ma says she's the type that looks down her nose at everyone; she calls her Lady Muck. Gwen's mam's so surprised to see you that she doesn't even invite you in. Gwen's dad comes to the door; he has a paintbrush in his hand and he's covered in splotches of paint.

'I love the hair,' he says to you, and holds the door open to let you and Liam come in. 'Gwen!' he calls. 'Gwe-en! I've got a surprise here for you.'

You hear the clatter of feet upstairs and the next thing Gwen's there on the stairs, same as ever, her knee-socks flopping around her ankles like flabby wellies; her black hair as shiny as patent leather. She stops and gawps, she doesn't seem sure for a sec that it's really you. It makes you feel shy. But then she launches down the stairs and lands on top of you, nearly squashing your guts out.

'How did you get here? Where's your mam? How long are you staying? Do you want to see my den?' she pulls you by the hand towards the stairs.

'Whoa, whoa, whoa,' her dad says. 'I think maybe we should all go into the living room and have a little chat.'

'I'm starving,' Liam says and Gwen's mam says she'll bring him into the kitchen to get something to eat. She gives her husband a long look. There are echoes all around the place and the boxes that went away in the truck from their house in Ireland are piled everywhere. It feels like Gwen has been gone forever, but seeing all their stuff still packed away makes you realise it's only been a few weeks.

'How long does it take for a letter to get from Ireland to Wales?' you ask, sitting down on a box. You feel awful tired.

'A couple of days; less than a week, anyway,' her dad says. 'Why do you ask?'

You swallow some spits and sigh. For the second time you have to tell all about what happened to the baby. It feels worse this time because Gwen and her parents knew him, but you are too tired to cry, so you just kind of whisper it out. Tears splash from Gwen's eyes on to the bare floorboards. You tell them how your da's girlfriend hates Liam and you are in charge of him, so you decided to get him out of there and go far, far away. And because Gwen had said in her letter that you were welcome any time, you thought that Wales would be far enough. You want to say something about Bella, but the words stay locked in your throat.

Nobody says anything. Gwen's mam comes in with a plateful of toast; Liam trails behind.

'Why all the long faces?'

Gwen's dad says, 'There's been an accident,' and he brings her out into the hall to tell her, so that you don't have to hear him saying it, but his words bounce back into the room on an echo. You hear him say 'Que sera, sera' which you know is Latin for 'bad things happen'. Gwen's da has been to a lot of countries and knows all the languages. He's a college teacher; that's why they came back to Wales, because of his job. Gwen's mam comes into the living room, still carrying the toast, which you would like a bit of, and her eyes are dripping with sad sympathy.

'You poor wee darlings,' she says, handing the plate to Gwen. Then she nearly breaks your skeleton in a hug. She's very strong. 'Let's get you each a long hot bath and then we'll eat properly.'

They ring your da; you give them the number, but you don't hear what they say. You lie back in the bath and let your ears fill with sudsy water, so that everything's muffled. The water closes around your skin like a heavy coat. Gwen comes into the bathroom and kneels on the floor beside the bath; you sit up. She reaches over and takes your hand, which means you can't wash yourself, but you stay like that for a few minutes, saying nothing.

'Best friends forever,' Gwen whispers and you nod your head.

8

In Wales

There are no curtains on the windows in Gwen's new house. The bed they give you is high and wide, and there's loads of room for you and Liam. Still, he snuggles over to your side, following you across the mattress. All of a sudden you aren't as tired as you were. You can hear voices thrumming downstairs through the hollowness of all the empty rooms. The moon casts a band of silver across the eiderdown; it's nice to be able to look out and see it like a clean white plate hanging in the sky. It makes you think of your ma. She loves the moon and the stars, and she can name some of them. You look out for the Big Dipper and there it is; it's upside down, letting all the darkness it had scooped up fall out. The sky's different in Wales.

Your teacher told your class before that there's no light from the moon; when you contradicted her, she got real flustery.

'Did I not just say that the moon does *not* throw any light?' She fisted up her hands until the knuckles went white.

'But Miss, I've seen it, Miss,' you said, half getting up out of your chair.

'Sit down and don't be so cheeky,' she said, and she gave you extra homework. You knew you were right and so did everyone else; sometimes teachers want to prove a point and show you who is boss.

You say a little prayer to Saint Philomena, asking her to keep an eye on your ma until you get to see her again. 'Dear Saint Philomena, please mind my ma. Keep her safe and well and happy,' you say in your mind. 'Amen.'

The morning creeps into the room very early. Gwen's dad calls you down for breakfast. He tells you that Geraldine has had her baby. It's a girl. You're glad it's not a boy, because you never want to know another boy baby as long as you live.

'A little sister,' Gwen's mam says, smiling.

'Not really,' you say.

'We already have half a sister,' Liam says. 'Her name's Clare and she never stops crying.' It's the most he's said in ages.

'Your daddy won't be able to come over for a day or two, but I told him that you were fine.' She puts on a sad face. 'They were frantic, you know.'

You shrug; maybe your da was a teensy bit worried, but you'd say that Geraldine was delighted to see the back of you. 'Peace at last' she probably said. In fact, you bet that she laughed her head off when your da wasn't listening and said 'Yippee' to herself a million times. Still, you hope she likes her new baby and that it's a bit happier in itself than Clare. Little babies are gorgeous, with their squinty eyes and hot smell; you love the way they're so cuddly.

Gwen keeps hugging you. She says that she never wants you to leave, that you'll be friends for all time, for sure.

'What about Olive? You went on about her for ages in your first letter.'

'Oh, she's alright, but she's not like you.'

Gwen's dad goes off to work. Her mam doesn't want to let you out of her sight, but she has to go to the shops for the messages. In the end she brings Liam with her and you are surprised because he's delighted to go. He holds her hand going out the front door. You and Gwen sneak some biscuits and go up to her den. She has two beanbags to sit on and even though they're soft, they're hard as well; they're amazing and really comfortable. The den has all Gwen's stuff in it: a telly, her piano, toys, a radio. But not her bed;

she has a different room for sleeping. The two of you wiggle your bums into the beanbags to find the most comfy spot.

Gwen's mam has given you nail varnish to try on. She keeps the little bottles of it in the fridge, so that it doesn't go off. She calls it nail polish, but in your experience polish is for shoes and it's black. She doesn't let you have her very good stuff, which is browny-red like dark chocolate; she gives you a bright red one instead. You always used to cut your ma's nails; she liked to keep them plain. She could do her right hand by herself, but not her left hand, so she'd get you to do them. She'd have to sit very still while you held her hand in your lap and sliced through each nail with the curvy scissors. They'd fall into your skirt like little cat claws; you'd have to hoosh them into the bin without dropping them onto the floor. Otherwise they'd stick to the bottom of your socks when you walked around. Your ma's nails have little white flecks in them and she says they're caused by diamonds that are stuck behind her nails, trying to get out. She cuts her toenails herself because they are a private matter. She has a thing about other people touching her feet; she doesn't like it.

You think about the way your ma calls Gwen's mam 'Lady Muck' and you hope she would take it back if she could see how sweet Gwen's mam's being to you and Liam. The nail varnish goes all over your fingers and it's a disaster; it looks like you're bleeding to death. But it smells lovely: like paint or something. In the end you and Gwen do each other's nails because it's too hard to do your own.

'Your mam must be so sad,' Gwen says.

'Yes,' you say, picking bits of raisin out of your teeth while trying not to smudge the nail varnish. The biscuits you took are called Fruit Shorties. You tell Gwen how your da calls them 'fly biscuits' because the raisins look the same as squashed flies. But they don't taste like them.

'Did you go to the funeral?'

'Yes.'

'What was it like?'

You think for a minute. 'We went to the church in black cars. They played that song "Amazing Grace" and everyone was crying. My ma was like a zombie and my da had to mind her. Geraldine had a face on her.'

'It must have been awful upsetting. Did you cry all the time?'

You nod. 'It was horrible, especially in the graveyard because that was the end, and we had to say to ourselves "We'll never see the baby again," but my da said I can pick the baby's headstone.'

'That'll be lovely.'

'I might pick one in the shape of a baby angel.'

Gwen reaches over and pats your hand. Her face is really serious and you suddenly feel like laughing. Next thing a giggle bursts out of you. Gwen does a little laugh through her nose and looks sideways at you. In another minute the two of you are rolling around on the beanbags nearly weeing your knickers because you're laughing so much. You don't even hear her mam come into the room.

'When you ladies are quite ready…' she says, her hands on her hips. But she's smiling. 'Lunch is on the table.'

You and Gwen tumble down the stairs and you think it's like being on holidays. They call dinner lunch in Wales and it's a chicken curry from a takeaway, which is something you never get at home. It tastes like the smell of a restaurant, but it's very nice; kind of burny. You think a bit of curry is tasty, but a lot would be too much. You're sure Liam will hate it, but he gobbles up the whole lot, like a little muck savage. He's so sloppy that there are bits of rice stuck all over his jumper and there's a ring of yellow around his mouth from the sauce. He embarrasses the life out of you sometimes.

After lunch, you have to take the nail varnish off with smelly remover because Gwen's mam is bringing you out in the car and she says you look like two streetwalkers, whatever that's supposed to mean. Gwen has to get a special uniform for her new school. You would love to wear a uniform, but your school doesn't bother having one.

There are loads of hills in Bangor. Your legs would break off if you had to walk up and down them every day. Luckily you are being driven. The shop for Gwen's uniform is posh; it's long, like a corridor, and there are walls and walls of dark wooden shelves. The carpet feels springy under your sandals. You and Liam sit on two high stools inside the door to wait.

'Which school?' the lady asks.

'Saint Deiniol's.'

'How many?'

'Oh, just the one. Just my wee daughter here,' Gwen's mam says, pushing her forward.

The lady starts measuring Gwen around the middle and down her legs and you all go into fits of the giggles. The lady looks very cross, as if she'd love to slap you, one by one.

'Do you want *everything*?' she snaps, and Gwen's mam says she supposes so, but she doesn't look sure.

You cross your eyes at Gwen and the lady goes off to get the stuff. She comes back with her arms full of clothes and she has another lady with her whose arms are loaded down as well. They are yapping away to each other in a foreign language, which turns out to be Welsh. It sounds kind of the same as Irish, except it's more like coughing. It takes Gwen ages to try on all the bits of the uniform; it includes a navy pinafore, a blue blouse, a stripey tie, a cardigan, a blazer, a coat, a pair of culottes, a sports shirt, a straw hat, and even special socks. But they don't make her try on the socks, thank God. The hat is gorgeous. It's like something that girls in a school in a comic would wear.

When everything's paid for, Gwen's mam piles the bags into the boot and says that you deserve a treat after all that. She brings the three of you to a place called The Fat Cat Café, which looks out over the water and two huge bridges – one called Britannia, for cars and trains, and the other called Telford's, for cars only. They're beautiful bridges – nicer even than the ones over the Liffey in town, except for the Ha'penny Bridge, which is the best in the world. Gwen says the water is called the Menai Straits and that it and the bridges separate the island of Anglesey from Bangor and the rest of north Wales. You say that Llanfair PG is on Anglesey and Gwen's mam's amazed at your knowledge.

'How do you know that?'

'Oh, I just heard.' You think it might be better not to say anything about Bella, because she's a stranger and you're supposed to steer clear of them.

The ice-cream menu has all sorts of lovely things, and in the end you have a Banana Split, Liam has a Knickerbocker Glory, and Gwen has a Strawberry Sundae. Her mam just has a coffee. Grown-ups are not that fond of ice cream. You all share a taste of each other's, but you're glad when the sharing's over, because you think yours is the nicest and you want to have it all to yourself. The bananas are covered in splodges of hot chocolate sauce and lots of cream.

'Your mammy must miss you both so much,' Gwen's mam says, licking the frothy milk off her coffee spoon. You look at her; she's pretty in an ugly kind of way. She has too many chins and bockety eyes, but her hair is nice: very dark and straight.

'And the baby,' Liam says.

'Yes, and the baby,' she says, cupping Liam's cheek in her hand. He grins and pokes the long spoon he has into the middle of his ice cream.

'I miss my mammy,' he says. 'I want to go home.'

You look out the café window. The water in the Menai Straits is being churned up by the wind, and the colour of it keeps changing from green to brown to grey. You decide that Telford's Bridge is your favourite of the two bridges; it's fancier than the other one and it goes on for ages, high up over the water. You wonder if it's safe; you could imagine it splitting open – all the pale steel girders pinging apart like broken guitar strings – and the cars tumbling into the soupy water.

'OK troops, let's mosey on. How about a trip to the pictures?'

You all start cheering and Gwen's mam has to tell you to shush. When you get to the cinema, the only film that's suitable for all of you is *The Empire Strikes Back*. It's an outer-space one and not your cup of tea, but you don't say anything. It turns out to be quite good though, because Luke Skywalker's handsome and Gwen's mam buys goodies: popcorn and sweets. She's turning out to be different to the Gwen's mam who lived near you at home; much better altogether.

You're all quiet in the car on the way back to Gwen's house because you're tired. You like watching Bangor sail past: the higgledy-piggle of houses and the boats in the harbour look lovely, but you can't stop thinking about home and your ma. She's the most beautiful woman in the world. Even when she's thin and pale and sad, she looks nice. You hope she gets well really soon; totally better. Being away from home's not as much fun as you'd think; there are lots of things to do and everyone's being kind and all, but still. And you have to say that Wales is great and very interesting, but it doesn't compare to Ireland or to Dublin or to your house by the river.

And nobody compares to your ma.

9

Unhappy Da

You lie in bed thinking that if you had to choose between two punishments, you can't decide which would be worse: to have to count every single blade of grass in the world, or to be hanged by the neck. At least if you were counting the blades of grass, you'd still be alive. But you'd hardly ever see your family, or get a chance to play or eat a proper meal or sleep. Being hanged would hurt, and there's a chance you mightn't die straight away and that would hurt even more. You'd be hanging there in front of everyone and your eyes would go all googly and your tongue would flop out the side of your mouth. Your neck would be in bits. Thinking about it keeps you awake for ages. It might be best to choose counting the grass as a punishment; at least while you were doing it in Ireland, your ma and da and Liam could visit, and even help out a bit, if that wasn't breaking the rules.

There's no moon out; it must be on its way to Australia. That's what your ma always says when the moon disappears. Your da's coming to take you and Liam back to Dublin. It will be great to see him, and to go on the ferry again, but you will miss Bella being there and the way she's so kind and gentle. You wonder if your da will buy you dinner in the restaurant on the boat. If you were him, you might be a little bit angry at you for running away, but you hope he won't be.

The door creaks open and it's Gwen. It turns out that she can't sleep either. You slide Liam over to the wall – he's fast asleep – and Gwen slips into the bed. Her feet are cold.

'I don't want you to go.' You don't want to lie to her and say that you don't want to go either, so you squeeze her fingers instead. 'I'll write to you every day,' she says, through a yawn. Then she falls asleep and you are squashed between two snorers; you're probably the only person still awake in the whole of Bangor – maybe even the whole of Wales.

Your da looks wrecked. His cheeks are like blue-grey eyes and the insides of his real eyes are all bloodshot like rhubarb. He's polite to Gwen's mam and dad, but you can tell that you're in for it by the way he's going on. He hardly says hello to you, but he gives Liam a proper big hug and kiss. His face is full of hurt when he looks at you, but mostly he doesn't even let your eyes meet. You know that that means he's crazy upset.

'They've been very well behaved,' Gwen's mam says, 'like little angels, really.'

Your da nods. 'Thanks for everything. I'm sorry.' He sighs; he keeps doing that, letting out these big mad sighs. You're getting a bit fed up of it; if it wasn't for his poxy girlfriend, you wouldn't have had to leave and he wouldn't have had to come all the way to Wales after you. So it's not your fault.

Everyone stands around in the hallway of Gwen's house, cluttering it up. You say goodbye to Gwen and she gives you a silver bracelet of hers as a present; it has a charm which is in the shape of a four-leafed clover.

'It's to bring you good luck,' Gwen says.

You look over at her mam and she nods, which means it's OK to take it. Gwen clips it on to your wrist. You promise to write. It seems to take ages to say goodbye and you wish it was over, so you could go. Liam gives her mam a kiss, and then they all stand at the gate and wave at you going off in the taxi. Your da starts the sighing again and he rubs at his eyes with his hands.

'Aren't you even going to ask how Geraldine and the new baby are?'

You don't say anything for a minute. 'What did she call it?'

'Lisa.'

'Oh.'

'Lisa-Schmisa-Pisa,' Liam says, but nobody laughs.

'Is that all you can say, "Oh"?' your da says. 'Do you have any idea what you put us through? Do you?' He slaps his hands off his knees. 'You're a selfish little brat! I can't believe it, after everything we've done for you.'

You can feel tears coming through the back of your eyes and trying to break out, but there's no way you're going to cry in front of him. You're the one who should be raging.

'Well, if it wasn't for Geraldine, we wouldn't –'

He cuts across you, wagging his finger in your face.

'Don't you dare try and blame Geraldine for this. She did everything she could for you and this is the thanks she gets! You steal from us and then you take your brother away, not leaving so much as a note. Geraldine has been sick with worry. Sick! And she has enough on her plate.' You shrug. 'It's your mother you should be looking at…' He doesn't go on, but closes his mouth up real tight, as if he's afraid the words might escape by themselves.

The ferry home's not much fun. Your da and Liam share a seat in the lounge, all pally-wally and mad about each other. You sit across from them, pretending you're not with them, and that seems to suit your da fine. The two of them are there with their arms around one another, talking and laughing. Well, your da's not laughing much, but he's smiling anyway. You decide to go for a walk around the deck, even though it's drizzling.

'Where do you think you're going?' your da says, the minute you stand up.

'For a walk.'

'You're not going anywhere, missy. Sit back down there.'

You plop back down on the seat and put on a puss, to let him know that you're not exactly happy with him either. He's not the only person entitled to go around being narky. Then your da comes over to you and you think he's probably full of remorse for his carry on. You put on an even sulkier face, so that he'll know you don't forgive him yet. He kneels beside your chair and, after a minute, you lift your eyes to him, but he's not even looking at you; he's staring over at the windows.

'Keep an eye on Liam, I'll be back in a sec,' he says, getting to his feet. Then he walks off. Liam comes over and squashes into your seat beside you. You push at him because he's taking up all the room. The ferry's much giddier in the water than it was on the way over. If you were walking around, it'd probably make you feel a bit sick. But you'll never know because you're stuck minding Liam. But really, you think, he's not so bad as a brother. You give him a dig with your elbow.

'Hey,' he yelps.

'Which would you rather do: run a mile, suck a boil, or eat a bag of scabs?' you ask him.

'Eughhhhhh!' Liam laughs and pokes you in the belly with his bony fingers. You poke him back.

'Well, which?'

'None of them,' he says.

'But you have to pick one.'

'Say them again.'

'Run a mile, suck a boil, or eat a bag of scabs.' You snuggle your bum into the seat to make more room for yourself. 'I'd run a mile, that'd be easy.'

'Me too,' says Liam, because he says everything you say.

'Copycat, copycat, one, two, three…'

'Leave your brother alone.' Your da's standing there, holding paper cups of tea and packets of sandwiches.

'But we were just –'

'No buts. Liam, come over here with me.' Your da settles Liam into the chair with a cheese sandwich and then he comes over to you. You don't dare say that you don't drink tea, especially seeing that it's not really true any more, since you drank some with Bella Larkin. He hands you your food and the hot paper cup, and then he sits back over with Liam. You all eat without speaking and the ferry dips through the waves towards Dún Laoghaire.

Geraldine's not home from the baby hospital yet. Clare's gone to stay with her Nana, which is another way to say granny, or in other words, Geraldine's ma. The flat's boiling hot, as usual. Your da's still in a bad mood with you, and a good mood with Liam. Any minute now he'll forget which mood he's supposed to be in. Then you'll laugh at him and he'll deserve it.

Sinbad goes banana-boats when he sees you through the balcony door. He hops up off his bed and starts firing himself against the glass until you let him in. He dances around your legs, yapping like a mad thing, and jumps up to sniff your fingers. You'd swear you'd been gone for half a century the way he's going on. You kneel down on the rug and let him lick your nose with his smelly tongue. That's how dogs kiss each other. Then you remember that they also lick each other's bums, so you don't let him do it any more. Still, at least someone's glad to see you.

Your da stands in the middle of the room watching. 'Pack up the rest of your stuff,' he says. 'You pack up Liam's things for him.'

Sinbad tries to snuggle on to your lap, but you push him away. You look up at your da.

'What? Why?'

'Cora's coming tomorrow to collect you both.'

'Merciful hour, you gave us all the fright of our lives,' Cora says, breaking every bit of you in a hug and letting you into the back seat of the Merc. You breathe in the car's lovely leathery smell.

'We thought we'd lost you,' Noel says, smiling into the rear-view mirror. 'And what would Noel do without his little Liamo?' He winks at you; Liam grins.

At first when your da said you had to go to stay with Cora, you weren't one bit happy. But now you're delighted because you don't have to look at his big moany head every minute and you won't have to listen to Clare or the new baby squawking when they come home to the flat. And you won't have to face Geraldine. Anyway, staying in Cora's house means the river's only a little walk away. You miss it. And it means that each second you're getting nearer to going home to your own house.

You feel warm in your belly when the car turns over the bridge and pulls up in front of Cora and Noel's house. All the trees look so leafy and bushy since you last saw them, and the buzz-buzz of someone's lawnmower is the exact sound of home. Cora makes the dinner and after you've eaten it all up, as well as biscuits and lemonade, you settle in front of the telly. It's late and there's only boring stuff on, like news and other talking. You twiddle the good-luck bracelet that Gwen gave you. Cora and Noel light up fags and you think some things never change, but you don't really mind. Cora says she has something to show you. She takes the newspaper out of Noel's hands while he's reading it.

'Hey,' says Noel.

'Hay is good for horses,' Cora says. 'You can have it back in a minute.' She holds the paper in front of you and points to a bit; she hands it to you and your eyes nearly pop out of your head when you read it:

'RUNAWAYS FOUND IN WALES' it says across the top of a little piece of writing. Then it goes on: 'Two children who went missing from their father's Dublin home on Thursday have been found unharmed in Bangor in north Wales. The two, a girl aged ten and a boy aged six, apparently took the ferry to Wales after a family row. They have now been reunited with their father and Gardaí are not seeking anyone in connection with their disappearance.'

You look up at Cora. Her face is serious, but it looks like a laugh might hop out of her mouth any second.

'We're famous,' you say.

'Hmmm,' Cora says, half-smiling, 'famous indeed. But anyway, all's well that ends well. Isn't that what they say, Noel?'

'That's right, love,' says Noel, holding his hand out for the paper.

You read the words through again. 'Can I keep it? Can I cut it out for my scrapbook?'

'Indeed and you can,' says Cora, giving the paper back to Noel, 'once His Lordship is finished devouring it.'

Liam's too small to understand that you are both famous and Very Important Persons now, or VIPs for short. It's a pity that they didn't put your names in the paper, then everyone you know would definitely know it was you. Or a photo; a picture of the two of you would've been better again. You can't wait to see Anne Brabazon's face when she finds out about this! She'll never be able to beat it. You wonder if your da saw it. It's typical of him to keep it a secret just to spite you, so that you wouldn't even know you were famous all over Ireland.

Then you wonder if your ma saw it too and if she was worried about you both. You hope not.

10

Seeing your Ma

Most of the baby's stuff's gone since the day your ma threw it all in the river. The only things you have left are a few jumpers and vests. And some photographs. Cora lets you go down to your own house when you feel like it; she says it'll do the place good to have people roaming around it again. You push the windows open wide to get clean air flowing through the rooms. Then you sort through the baby's things, moving them from the top to the bottom drawer in your ma's chest of drawers. His towelling vests feel snuggly on your face and they smell like washing powder. You miss the baby so much; it's as if there's a hole dug out of your body where he used to live and nothing can fill it up.

You want to make a present for your ma; Cora says she'll give you a hand. You take the shoebox that holds the photographs of you all out from under your ma's bed: there's pictures of her and your da and the baby and Liam and you. There's some in there of your granny and granda when they were alive, and of your auntie Bridget and your uncles, who you never see much. They all look so different; young and happy. Your ma always says she'll get around to putting them in an album one day. You put the best photo of the baby in a silver frame that Cora gives you; it's a picture of him in his pram, smiling up at the camera and showing his new teeth. His cheeks look soft and brown. You leave that picture beside her bed, the frame shining and the baby looking so healthy, cheerful and alive.

Then you and Cora stroll up to her house with the shoebox and sit at the kitchen table. You take some of the other photos and stick them onto the back of a Weetabix box. You put the ones of the baby in the middle; then photos of Liam all around them; and lastly the ones of you, because you are the eldest. It's called a montage; you made one in school before, with old birthday cards. Your teacher's mad into making stuff. Liam thinks it's gorgeous. Cora promises to buy a big frame to hold it and she says you can bring it up to the hospital to give to your ma.

'Just wait until Joan sees that; she'll be only delighted.'

'Do you really think she'll like it?'

'I don't just think it, I *know* it,' Cora says, putting away the scissors and glue.

'Cora, I wish you were our auntie instead of Bridget.'

'That's a shocking thing to say; your poor auntie Bridget!' Cora says, grabbing you and Liam in a hug and laughing. But you know she doesn't really mean it; she wishes that she was your auntie too. Even though Cora and Noel are fat and wobbly, and they smoke too much, you think they're great.

Anne Brabazon calls for you. She asks if you want to go out and play skipping. You say you'd rather hang around outside. Cora says it's alright to go, but not to be too long and to stay well away from the river.

The sun's bursting in and out from behind the clouds. One second it's cold and the next it's roasting. You pull your jumper on when the sun goes in again.

'Your hair's nice,' Anne says.

'Oh, yeah,' you say, patting it down with your hand. Anne's ma will never let her get her hair cut, even though she's a hairdresser herself. That's because Anne has to have it long for the Irish dancing, to make into ringlets that bounce when she dances. It's all part of the look; it goes with the lovely embroidered dress and the poodle-socks and the poms.

'I'd love to have a pageboy,' Anne says, 'but my ma won't let me.'

'I know,' you say, swishing your head a little bit to emphasise your nice hairdo.

'You were in the paper.' You look down at your toes peering out of the tops of your sandals.

'Oh, that?'

'Did you really run away?' Anne's eyes are as wide as two flying saucers.

'Yeah; all the way to Gwen's new house in Wales. It's a mansion.'

The two of you walk down towards the bridge. Cora said not to go near the river, but you're sure it's OK if you stay up on the bridge. You and Anne throw sticks into the rushing water and then run across to the other side to watch them float through. The river's high and it carries the sticks fast, but some of them get lost.

'How many rooms are in Gwen's mansion?'

'Oh, I don't know; about a hundred.' You plop a big stick into the water and run over to wait for it. Anne follows you.

'You're a lucky sucker. I'd love to go on a trip like that.'

'It was brilliant.'

Anne twiddles her hair through her fingers and looks at you. 'I hear your ma's back in the loony.'

You lean over the bridge and stare down at the water; the stone wall cuts into your chest and makes your breath raggy. The stick comes bouncing through, followed by bits of weed and scurfy stuff. Anne's one must have got stuck. You turn to face her and put your hands on your hips.

'For your information, my ma is *not* a loony.' You waggle your finger at her nose and she leans back to get away from it. 'But your ma's a stupid bitch and *everyone* knows it!' You shout the last bit at her and then you turn and walk away, real calm. Only, on the inside, you're all twisted up; your guts are grabbing at each other. Halfway up the road you bend down, pretending to fix the buckle on your sandal; you take a sneaky look back through your legs at Anne. She's still standing on the bridge; the sun is shining through her yellow hair and it looks like a halo around her head. For some reason that makes you cry and you walk back to Cora's house full of sadness. Cora's out the back, sitting on a deckchair, sunning her lumpy legs. Her straw hat flops over her eyes.

'When are we going up to Saint Jude's to see my ma?'

It's raining; huge showers splash out of the sky every ten minutes or so and then leave again. It's so heavy that it looks false, like sheets of needles falling, or like the kind of rain you see on the telly. Steam rises off the road in between the showers. You and Cora are on the bus, going to the hospital; your skirt's damp and so is everyone on the bus. There's a hot, wet smell off everything. You can hardly see out the window, the way the rain's rivering down it. Noel's minding Liam; he's brought him out in the coal truck to collect the money from the customers. On another day, you would've liked to go too, but Noel says they'll be all done in half an hour because no one wants to buy coal during the summer. You're glad for Noel that the weather has turned bad.

Luckily, by the time you and Cora get off the bus, the sun's out again. Some of the patients are walking in a group in the grounds of the hospital when you get there; they walk real slow and none of them looks at the others.

'It's depressing,' Cora says, rolling her umbrella up into a tight sausage and making a face, 'the poor divils don't know whether they're coming or going.' Big drips fall from the trees as you pass under them. You know that if you shook the branches hard, it would make a really heavy rain, the kind that drops down inside your collar and wets your neck. Cora scuttles you on towards Hospital Two and Saint Philomena's wing. The group of patients are still walking along, but one of them has stopped and is staring over at you. You do a tiny wave and she waves back. 'Don't be encouraging them,' Cora says. 'The craythurs.'

You walk backwards down the corridor in your ma's wing, to make sure Philomena's still on her perch, looking out for everyone there and, most of all, for your ma. She is. Cora tells you to stop foostering about and to walk properly.

'This whole place gives me the heebie-jeebies,' she says.

'What's that?' you ask, as they let you through the gate to get to where your ma is.

'You know, it gives me the willies; the creeps,' she says, doing a full body shiver.

'The willies!' You do a little laugh because Willy is your da's name. Then you get to your ma's door and you don't feel like laughing any more. It's closed, same as the last time. The two of you look at each other, then Cora knocks gently on the door.

'Come in.'

You twist the door handle and let yourself in; the room's bright, sun glowing through the window. A warm smell blasts into your face, it's like stale perfume and sweat and mint. It takes a minute for you to see properly; you look over towards your ma's bed. It's empty.

'Hello there,' says a voice from across the room. There's a girl sitting on the other bed, her legs are tucked up and crossed over. She has long red hair that curls on the ends; you think she looks very young to be a nut-job.

'Oh, we're sorry to disturb you,' Cora says, 'we're looking for Mrs Joan Dunne?'

'Joan's with Dr Monahan,' the girl says, scrunching her nose, 'but she shouldn't be too much longer.' Then she closes her eyes, makes pincers with her fingers, and puts her hands on her turned-up knees. 'Hmmmmm,' she says, 'hmmmmm.'

Cora throws her eyes up to heaven and pushes you out the door; she shuts it quietly behind her. 'Jesus, Mary and Joseph, the sooner we get your ma out of this nut-house, the better.' You sigh and Cora grips her mouth into a tight shape.

Then you see her. She's shuffling down the corridor towards you, her arms folded across herself, holding her cardigan in place. Her hair's tied back into a sloppy ponytail and she comes slowly, slowly, following her feet with her eyes. You want to call out, shout 'Ma, it's me! I'm here! Look Ma, I'm here!', but the words get backed up in your throat. Cora and you stand outside the room, hearing the 'Hmmmmm-ing' from your woman inside, watching your ma snailing towards you. She lifts her eyes when she's nearly beside you and when she sees you, she stops.

'Oh.' The word pops from her lips.

'Ma,' you whisper and step forward. She lets her arms drop to her sides and her face crinkles up. Then she lifts her arms to you and you fall forward into them. 'Oh, Ma.'

'There's a good girl,' she whispers into your hair, 'there's a great girl.' She smells like herself; sweet like soap and lavender. You hold onto her, feeling her skinniness under her clothes.

'Come on now,' says Cora, 'the two of you will have me in floods; let's go somewhere and sit down.'

You pull back from your ma and she pets your cheek. 'How are you doing, Little Miss Prim?' Her fingers are cool.

'I'm grand, Ma.'

'And Liam?'

'He's grand too. He's dying to see you.'

She does a weak smile and hugs you to her side. 'Good, good.' She looks at Cora. 'There you are, Missus.' She sounds like Winnie, the way she says that.

'God, Joan, you're looking marvellous,' say Cora, her eyes all swimmy. She grabs your ma's hand and waggles it.

'I'm feeling much better.' She doesn't look too marvellous at all; her eyes are red, she's so skinny, her trousers look floppy, and she's paler than a raw potato. But she's a lot more human-looking than she was and that's the main thing. You were afraid she'd act all mental again this time, but she's being great. 'We'll go to the day room for a cup of tea; Susie is probably busy meditating on her bed again.'

'Is that what you call that?' Cora says. 'I'd just call it madness.'

Your ma turns to look at her and Cora's face goes pink.

'Oh, sorry,' she says, but your ma smiles at her and that's that.

'Come on, we'll have that tea and you can tell me all about your adventures in Wales.' You turn and stare at her. 'Don't look so surprised; your da told me. He had no choice.'

She links you on one side and Cora on the other, and the three of you walk down the clean, shiny corridor to the day room. In your mind you say a quick prayer to Saint Philomena, to say thanks very much for minding your ma so well. You think you might have a devotion to Saint Philomena, even though you don't really believe in God or any of that stuff.

You tell your ma all about Bella Larkin and how she was so nice to you and Liam. She says she will have to ring her up and say 'Thanks very much' and maybe even invite her for a visit to your house. You give her the framed photo-montage of the baby and Liam and you; she does a crying-smile, which is one that holds back tears.

'Thank you,' she mouths, but no sounds come from her lips.

11

A Homecoming

There are no cushions on the sofa since the time your ma threw them out through the window into the river and they floated away to the sea, or down to the river-bed, or somewhere else. Maybe they're stuck in the river-weed below your kitchen window. Because you can't sit on the sofa, you and your da sit on the mat on the floor in the sitting room to talk. His face is dead serious.

'You know I love you very much, don't you?' Cora has lit the fire and your face is getting very warm from it; you put your hand up to shield your cheek from the flames. 'You and Liam mean the world to me. And so do Clare and baby Lisa. I love each one of my kids and I worry about you all.' He's kind of mortifying you now and you're being baked alive by the fire. Cora wants the house sparkling for your ma coming home; she's been Mr Sheen-ing and tidying up all morning. Even the lino in the kitchen had to be scrubbed. By you. But you did it happily because it's all for your ma. 'So when you ran away I was out of my mind with worry. Do you understand?'

'Yes.' You wiggle away from the fire a little bit and try to look sorry.

'I was angry with you. You put yourself and Liam in terrible danger, whether you know it or not.' He scratches his cheek; he must be getting too hot as well. 'Luckily nothing happened; I mean nobody tried to...do anything to you, but anything could have gone wrong.'

'I know.' Your bum is getting sore; the mat's not exactly cushiony.

'Anyway, what I'm trying to say is, I was upset with you when I went to pick you up in Wales. Even though I was delighted to know you were safe and well, I was still furious with you. Do you understand why?'

'Yes.'

'Well, the thing is, I'm not sorry for being annoyed with you, but I suppose I'm a bit sorry for not letting you know how relieved I was that you were OK.' Your da sighs. 'So, I'm sorry for being cranky and I want you to know that we're all so glad to have you back, safe and sound.'

'Yes, Da.'

'But you have to promise me that if you're upset about anything ever again, you'll come and talk to me, or to your ma. You have to promise me that you'll never, ever pull a stunt like that again. It's important; say it now.'

'I promise, Da.'

He nods. 'Well good. Now, from here on in, yourself and Liam will be spending every other weekend with myself and Geraldine and the girls.' You whip your head up to look at him. 'I've spoken to Geraldine and I've spoken to your ma and everyone agrees. It'll give your ma a break and it'll help you to get to know the rest of your family. Because they *are* your family, you know.'

'But Geraldine doesn't like us; she especially hates Liam.'

'She does like you; she doesn't hate anyone,' he says gently. 'Look, she was in bad form when you stayed, that's true, but being heavily pregnant can make women feel very tired and sort of crabby. She's sorry for the way she went on.'

You hope you never get pregnant. 'OK,' you say, but you're not sure. Then you think for a minute and you have to admit that Geraldine can be alright sometimes. Like the time she brought you to Róisín's house to get your pageboy haircut, and the way she always gave you stamps and paper when you needed them. Anyway, you agree to give it a try, for your da's sake.

'And we'll look into those gymnastics classes you're so mad into doing; I believe they run them in our local parish hall.' He does a big happy smile.

'Da?' you say.

'What is it, honey?'

'Can I get up off the floor now? My bum-bones are killing me and the fire's too hot.'

'Go on,' he says, and you hop up to help Cora in the kitchen, where she's making sandwiches for your ma's homecoming party.

'There you are,' she says.

You stop by the kitchen window. It's pelting rain and the river water's fast-moving and all churned up. You wonder how your ma's going to feel, being back. You drag your finger along the window-pane and it makes a rubber-squeaky noise.

'Come on now, missy, less dreaming and more work,' says Cora. You turn around and she hands you a knife and a bowl of tomatoes. 'Cut them up into tiny little pieces and then do that cucumber; your ma loves a fresh salad sandwich.'

Your da comes into the kitchen; he stays in the doorway for a minute, watching you and Cora at work.

'I'll just go up to your house, Cora, to ring and arrange a taxi for Geraldine and the girls.'

'Right so, Willy; we're all dying to see your new baby – little Lisa.'

'She's a dote.' He grins.

You smile at your da. 'I can't wait to see my new sister,' you say and he comes over and gives you a backwards hug; a bone-crusher. Then he goes off out the door to ring for the taxi. You chop the tomatoes and their seedy juice slops all over the place. Cora turns on the radio and starts crowing away to the songs from the olden days that she loves so much.

The house is jammers; people are nearly tripping over one another and there aren't enough chairs.

'God, I hope we did the right thing,' Cora says. The party was her idea. 'I hope this isn't all too much for her.'

'She'll be delighted,' Winnie says, squeezing Cora's arm.

Winnie and Pa have brought loads of bottles of beer and lemonade, even though they are poor. Your auntie Bridget and Uncle Jack don't arrive with anything, but then Bridget sends Rory up to the shop for a few packets of biscuits. She pretends they didn't have time to stop along the way. Winnie raises her eyebrows to you. Rory's being all nice, smiling and grinning, and you can't believe it. Maybe he got a brain transplant since you last saw him.

The house looks great. It's really neat and tidy, everything dusted, shiny and wiped. Cora took down all the curtains and washed them, so there's an extra fresh feeling. Even the mice are gone because your da got a man in to murder every last one of them. You feel sorry for the mice in one way, but in another way you're glad, because it's not funny to find poo pellets in the food press and cereal boxes that have been chewed up, or that kind of thing. Your ma'll be happy that they're gone.

Noel's gone to collect your ma in the green Merc; she'll be home soon. Winnie and Cora have put a tablecloth on the table, and all the food's spread out, ready for your ma. There are butterfly buns and coconut buns, big fat sausage rolls and teeny cocktail saussies, tons of different kinds of sambos like chicken, salad and ham; there are apple tarts and rhubarb tarts, chocolate biscuits and pink spongey ones, bowls of crisps and peanuts. The beer and fizzy lemonade is in the fridge. But best of all is the cake that Cora got made at a bakery in town. It has white icing that's as smooth as new snow and in red swirly letters it says 'Welcome Home, Joan'. You can't wait to get a taste of it. You and Liam made a poster for the hall that says 'Ma'. It's huge and you painted lovely blue forget-me-nots on it, to show her that you never forgot about her when she was gone away to the hospital. Everyone says it looks terrific – a real work of art – and you agree.

Geraldine arrives with Clare and the baby; she gives you a kiss, but she doesn't give out or say she was worried or anything like that. Your da probably told her about your chat. She looks lovely in the pale pink dress she's wearing. Clare's amazingly quiet. The baby's tucked into one of those soft nests, which looks like a miniature sleeping bag. Geraldine holds her out for you to see.

'Say hello to Lisa,' she says, 'your baby sister.' You look at her and you can't believe how teeny tiny she is; especially because Geraldine was so fat when Lisa was inside her. She's beautiful: sort of reddish-pink with a wincy little nose. Her hand's sticking out the top of the baby-nest and you are amazed to see that she has long, long fingers and mauve-coloured nails.

'She's gorgeous,' you whisper, and Geraldine says you can hold her later, after she's been fed and changed. You nod and offer to get Geraldine a cup of tea. She sits into the sofa, which Cora has lined with pillows and covered with a sheet. It turns out it's very comfortable. Liam squashes in beside Geraldine and he can't take his eyes off the baby; he slips his finger into her hand and little Lisa holds onto it while she sucks away on her soother. Liam's thrilled with Lisa.

'They're here!' someone sings out, and you all rush to the windows and the door. The Merc pulls up in front of the house. The rain has eased off a bit; it's drizzling. Noel jumps out and holds an umbrella up for your ma; you're proud of him for being so gentlemanly. She takes her time getting out of the car and looks around at everything. She says something to Noel and he nods. You're all staring out, breathing quietly; it's like watching a film in slow motion. Then your ma turns towards the house and, when she sees all the faces peeping out at her through the windows, her hand flies up to cover her mouth like she's in shock. Noel was supposed to tell her about the party, so she wouldn't have a heart attack when she walked in the door, but maybe he forgot. Your ma pushes her hands through her hair and starts to cry. People start to mumble and move back from the windows.

'It's all too much for her to take in, the poor peteen,' Winnie says. 'We shoulda known better.'

'She'll be OK,' your da murmurs.

Your ma walks into the sitting room. She looks beautiful: her hair's loose and she's wearing a custard-yellow t-shirt and her denim skirt. Tears are dribbling down her cheeks and she nods at everyone and says hello to a few different people. She's crying and laughing at the same time. When she sees Liam, she flops to her knees on the mat and holds her arms wide to him. Liam's still letting baby Lisa hold his finger. He stares at your ma for a second and then he unhooks Lisa's hand, slides off the sofa and runs to her. Liam jumps into her arms and she holds him to her, swaying this way and that.

'I missed you, Mammy. A lot.'

'And I missed you too, little pudding,' she says, sobbing like a mad thing in front of everyone. But it turns out half of them are crying too, so it doesn't really matter.

'Sit down here, Joan,' Geraldine says, trying to haul herself out of the sofa.

'Stay where you are,' your ma says and she sits down beside her. 'Can I?' she asks, holding out her arms for the baby. Geraldine hands Lisa over. Your ma dips her head and kisses the baby's soft cheek. 'Congratulations,' she says, smiling at your da and Geraldine. They both nod and smile back. Cora hands your ma a hanky and she blows her nose; it makes a hooty noise and everyone laughs.

'Let's get this show on the road,' Noel says, rubbing his hands together. That means he wants to drink some beer, so you go into the kitchen to get him a bottle from the fridge.

You stop to look out the window; the rain has started up again.

It's rilling down the pane, bringing the cold in, taking every sign of the summer away. You push the window wide and hang out over the windowsill to watch the river spinning past; the rain plops into it and becomes a part of the splashing, foaming water. The air feels a little cool on your face. There's a blue-and-white-striped plastic bag stuck in a tree on the opposite bank. The wind pulls at it, and it shakes and balloons out; you think you can hear it rustle, even above the gushing, rushing noise of the weir.

The kitchen door opens, so you pop your head back in from watching the river to see who's there.

It's your ma. She folds her arms and smiles at you, so you smile back. You think she looks happy to see you. You're certainly happy to see her.